SHEPLER'S SPRING

SHEPLER'S SPRING

Lauran Paine

GUNSMOKE

First published in the UK by Hale

This hardback edition 2009
by BBC Audiobooks Ltd
by arrangement with
Golden West Literary Agency

ISBN 978 1 405 68287 9

British Library Cataloguing in Publication Data available.

Printed and bound in Great Britain by
CPI Antony Rowe, Chippenham and Eastbourne

"YOU SON OF A BITCH!"

He came out of Black Rock Desert to Pyramid Lake, camped a week because his horse was sore-footed, then turned north-east in the direction of the Humboldt River seeking a town where he could get shoes for the animal, and the only two-legged life he saw was in the tules around Pyramid Lake where some squatty, moon-faced, lank-haired aboriginal Piute squaws had been seed gathering. They had not seen him, he had been careful about that, but after he left, tribesmen probably had encountered his tracks because they undoubtedly lived around the lakeshore. They were grub eaters. They would lick their forearms and hands then shove the hand into an anthill. When the ants were swarming over the saliva-covered arm, the Piutes would then lick them off.

Frontiersmen called them "diggers" because they dug for insects, roots, occasionally buried offal where a train of wagons had passed by. They were dim witted, surly and treacherous. They were bad hunters and poor warriors. If they hadn't been, they would no doubt have broken out of the desert where other tribesmen had chased them, and had never bothered to go back in there to raid or liquidate them.

No one else wanted the desert. The Diggers did not want it either, but they were unable to take and hold anything better.

They *did* find the tracks, puzzled over them because the horseshoe imprints were thin and broken, and the boot-prints showed low heels and no spur-drag. But the rider had been gone several days by the time they wrapped their bodies in tied tules, covered arms and faces with mud, and began stealthily to stalk the tracks with their stubby little primitive bows and arrows. The only way they killed was by murder, but this time all their preparations were in vain.

The rider was in fact, about the time the Piutes were sneaking up on the rock pile where he'd camped, sitting in shed-shade outside a blacksmith's works in a place no larger than a freighter camp which was called Shepler's Spring, or just Shepler, Nevada Territory.

To the burly, dark-visaged taciturn horseshoer with the keen grey eyes the flat-heeled stranger was another drifter. They came and went. Not very often because Shepler's Spring was out of the cattle country, there were no mines nearer than the heat-blurred bluish mountains. Except for the spring, the abundance of water around Shepler which had drawn freighters and stagers like a magnet since the early days, there was little to attract people.

But that fine, blue-water spring had encouraged the hamlet to take root, and while it was not a large place, scarcely even deserving the name of a ' town ', it had

6

a saloon, a general store, a smithy, a large stage-company corralyard, and a big flat area on the east side of town with an *acequia*, where freighters camped on their way through.

It also had a chest-high mud fort, dilapidated now, where a stray column of soldiers had once bivouaced, and where the Diggers had come squirming on their bellies like snakes to launch an attack, not because they hated soldiers—they scarcely knew what a blue-belly was—but they loved horsemeat.

A century hence a historical society would erect a bronze tablet there. By then the fort would have dissolved completely leaving not even a rim of vague mounds. The tablet would commemorate a heroic stand of horse infantry against an enlightened, fierce and colourful foe.

But while that lean man was sitting in the shed-shade waiting for his horse to be shod so he could push onward, that fight was still fairly fresh in folks' minds. The Diggers had loosed a shower of wobbly arrows made of tules, had sprang to their feet to howl and make a run at the mud fort, the soldiers had turned out with their stubby trapdoor Springfields, and when the rank smoke had lifted there were eleven dead Piutes and about thirty others running in all directions as hard as they could flee, unimpeded in most cases by britches or breech-clouts.

That was the whole campaign.

There was an old pad-saddle lying indifferently at the base of a slovenly old cottonwood tree outside the smithy, which the waiting stranger studied with casual interest, and when the blacksmith straightened up to drink from his hanging *oll*a and saw the younger man's interest he said, " It ain't local. I got it in a trade with some surveyors—army surveyors—who came through Shepler six, seven years ago."

The lean stranger nodded. " Blackfeet," he said. " That surveying party must have come from Montana or Wyoming."

The unsmiling blacksmith swept a hairy forearm across his whiskered lips, draped the *olla* back on its peg, eyed the younger man with steady interest, said nothing more and returned to his work.

The country was flat, mostly sandy loam since this was springtime it was green, in a pale way, irregularly speckled by patches of red and gold, pink and deep violet where wild flowers grew.

The town had trees but elsewhere as far as a man could see it was a timberless countryside, open, flat, with visibility crystal-clear for at least a hundred flat miles in all directions. The Tonopahs stood north-easterly, crumpled cardboard mountains with little to recommend them, outwardly anyway, although miners picking and scratching up there had found gold, silver, and a number of other metals for which there was no market at all—yet.

The stranger removed his stiff-brimmed, flat-topped hat, settled back with rawboned shoulders against the rough wall of the shoeing shed, shoved out sinewy legs and studied the town. Clearly, if a road had not curved around through Shepler's Spring because of the water in this essentially waterless territory, there would be no town here.

He watched an old man with a fat old black dog amble from between two buildings in the direction of a warped and weathered old bench out front of the corralyard, and sit down in the sunshine over there. The old dog was grey above the eyes and down around the muzzle, and when the old man spoke the dog did not look around. Deaf, or nearly so.

They were a pair. The stranger guessed the old man to be in his seventies; late seventies and maybe more. A burly dark man strode through the corralyard gates, saw the old man, said something, and when the old man slowly turned, the burly dark man swore. This, the stranger heard. The old man started to rise, but he was long past the age when he could move swiftly. The burly man took two steps, grabbed, heaved the old man to his feet, then turned and viciously kicked the completely unsuspecting old dog.

The man staggered but the dog went down, threshing and making a coughing sound in his chest.

In one lithe movement the stranger came up off the seat in front of the shoeing shed and started up there in wide strides. Maybe the burly dark man had a reason for not wanting the old man sitting on the way-station bench, but the dog had not done anything.

The old man was shivering as he turned to lean and reach a hand for the old dog. Neither he nor the burly man heard anyone behind them until the lanky stranger reached, whirled the burly man and said, "You son of a bitch!" and hit him so hard the burly man's hat sailed into the wide roadway.

The burly man went sprawling, rolled over, scrabbled in roadway dirt with bent fingers, then fell forward as the stranger stepped past and knelt to look at the old dog. There was blood, he looked up, baffled, from rheumy, old, hurting dark eyes.

The stranger probed, felt the broken ribs, rocked back on his heels as the old man began mumbling something, and looked around. Down at the shoeing shed the blacksmith was standing like a grim stone statue looking but neither making a sound nor moving. Across in front of the general store two men were also standing perfectly motionless staring.

The stranger stood up, glanced at the unconscious man in the dirt, then asked the old man where he lived, saying he would carry the dog home for him. The old man, confused and bewildered, pointed and shifted around his dog, then pointed again.

They walked away, the old man shuffling anxiously ahead, the rawboned younger man carrying the old dog whose breathing was shallow and whose eyes batted open and closed.

Finally, that pair of men in front of the store walked out and flopped the burly man onto his back, then stared. One of them said, " Gawddamn; he must've used a lead pipe. I've seen Manuel in a dozen fights but I never seen him put down before—and out cold like this."

The second man said nothing. He leaned, got the unconscious man sitting, then growled. It required all their combined strength to lift the inert man and get him back inside the corralyard.

The blacksmith took another drink from his *olla,* tied the shod horse in the shade alongside his shed, then removed his apron and went out front to sit in cottonwood shade and roll a smoke. The stranger never should have helped old Hap Sunday home, he should have come back, got on his black horse and headed out without stopping for fifty miles. Manuel Fuentes, the corralyard boss at Shepler's Springs for the Nevada Stage & Cartage Company, had an unpredictably bad disposition, and a reputation for violence which went all the way up to Virginia Dale near the Wyoming line where he had ridden with the most notorious way-station outlaw of them all, Jake Slade.

The blacksmith was impassively relaxed and smoking when the saloon proprietor came along looking worried. "Where'd that feller with the flat hat go?" he asked.

"Carried Hap Sunday's dog home for the old man," stated the blacksmith looking up. "Did you see it?"

"No. Just when those drivers picked Manuel up. What did this feller hit Manuel with?"

"His fist."

The saloonman pursed his lips. "Must be a hell of a big man, Henry."

The shoer shook his head. "Ain't no taller'n you are, Simon, and wringin' wet won't weigh more'n maybe a hunnert and seventy-five pounds."

" Who is he ? "

" I got no more idea than the man in the moon,"
replied the blacksmith, jerking his thumb. " That's his
black horse tied yonder." The blacksmith remembered
something. " I'd say he's from somewhere up north,
maybe Wyoming or Montana. And he's been a long
while on the trail. That horse didn't have nothin' more
than splinters of steel left on his feet."

The saloonman twisted to look around. The wide
roadway was empty, as it commonly was this time of
day; there would not be a stage through until mid-
afternoon. The morning coach had left Shepler before
sunrise, on schedule southward in the direction of Carson
City which lay just south of Virginia City.

" Someone better find that feller," said the saloonman, " and tell him to get out of here as fast as he
can."

The blacksmith killed his smoke underfoot. " Too
late," he said. " Manuel'll be coming around about now.
He'll be out in the roadway in a few minutes, and that
stranger's got to come right down the road from Hap's
shack to get down here to get his horse." The blacksmith raised gold-flecked amber eyes. " That's why I'm
sitting here, Simon. You might as well set down and
watch too."

2

GUNS!

Hap Sunday had been an army scout, a buffalo hunter, a trapper and mustanger, but all those things had used up a goodly portion of his years long ago. Now, he lived in an abandoned shack out behind town on the east side, his only companion that old dog, which he had found starving and sick ten years earlier.

They were a part of Shepler, their routine in spring and summer rarely varying; they sought sunshine to sit in. Old Hap occasionally earned a little money sweeping out the saloon, and Henry Shepler had him rake the shoeing shed floor now and then.

The shack smelled the way most hovels where forgetful old men lived. It was dim inside so the stranger had to wait, to become accustomed to the gloom—and the sour scent—before he and the old man made up a comfortable pallet for the old dog.

Hap's confusion remained. It had become a permanent condition gradually, over the last ten or so years. He always felt afraid without having any idea what he feared. Now, as the sinewy stranger made a thorough examination of the old dog, Hap got stiffly to his feet and shuffled in among some old boxes, groping and mumbling, and returned with a dusty whiskey bottle which he handed to the younger man.

"It'll help," he suggested. The younger man rocked back to study Hap, then he smiled, trickled a few drops into the dog's slack mouth, handed back the bottle and said, "Keep him warm. Don't let him move if you can help it. Cover him at night. Do you have some soft food?"

Hap nodded. "Mush. We make up a potful a couple times a week."

The younger man's steady grey eyes drifted around the hovel, then back to Hap. "What did that feller say to you before he kicked your dog?"

"Said for me not to sit on the bench. Said it was for stage passengers only. Said he didn't want my dog hoistin' a leg on the building and told me to get away. I was trying . . . I was gettin' up to go. I didn't want any trouble with Manuel . . . But Colonel, he was just sitting there. He hadn't done anything."

The younger man said, "What's your name?"

"Hap Sunday. Folks know me around Shepler's Spring. I been here quite a spell. Mind if I ask your name, mister?"

The younger man arose. "Bob Bryce." He leaned and patted Hap's shoulder. "I'll be back, Hap. Remember now, keep Colonel still, and feed him just soft stuff."

Outside, the sunshine was just as brilliant, a little time had elapsed but not much, the village was quiet, but it had been quiet before, Bob Bryce went down the

14

cluttered, unkempt alleyway on the east side of town, found a gloomy—and smelly—dogtrot between the general store and the harness works, stepped in and paced up it until he had a good view of the sunbright roadway out front, then he waited a moment, stood a long time in shadows considering the three men over in front of the corralyard polegate where they commanded full view of the road both ways. Two were armed with shotguns. The one called Manuel, with a purplish, lopsided appearance to his face on the left side, had the tie-down hanging loose on his holstered Colt. They were waiting.

No one else seemed to be in the roadway, at least until Bob Bryce craned southward he saw no one. There were two men sitting in tree-shade out front of the shoeing shed. One he recognized as the blacksmith. The other man was a stranger to him. They seemed to be simply relaxing, perhaps waiting to see what might happen, but in any case neither of them had a gun showing.

Bryce turned back down through, emerged in the alley and went all the way down to the lower end of town, waited until the opportunity occurred to get across the road unseen, then he went up as far as the shoeing shed by way of the west-side back alley.

He heard the smith and his friend out front talking quietly. His saddle outfit was still up-ended where he had put it. He drew forth the saddlegun, cracked the slide to verify what he was confident of, then started on out the front of the shop.

The smith and his companion looked up stunned into voiceless immobility. Bryce ignored them, watched those three armed men northward on the same side of the road, walked out away from the shed, out of tree-shade and swung the carbine into a two-handed grip as he cocked it waiting for someone up there to look southward.

One of them did, and hissed some kind of warning on an outrush of breath. Manuel Feuntes turned with his right hand dipping, his shoulder and arm blending with the speed and ease of the abrupt movement. Those other two with their scatterguns were helpless. With shotguns in both hands they had to get rid of those weapons before they could streak for their holsters. They stood very little chance.

Fuentes was fast. He fired from a low hold, using his triggerfinger to hold the trigger constantly depressed while he raised and dropped the hammer with his thumb-pad. It was an experienced, professional thing to do. But Manuel Fuentes should have been two hundred feet closer because his kind of draw was for killing across a card table, or no more than the width of a roadway.

He missed. The distance was too great and his draw was never meant for accuracy. He missed that one, and dropped the hammer a second time, as the sinewy man at the lower end of town raised his Winchester, took aim and fired.

Fuentes's entire body was punched sideways under impact. He was an oak-legged man, barrel-like, and solid bone and muscle. He took that bullet high up, and while a lighter, smaller man would have fallen, Manuel Fuentes staggered, stumbled a little, then began untracking his feet to face the gunman who had shot him.

Bryce spread his legs, kept the carbine snugged back, kept his finger curled, and when he saw Fuentes raising the handgun again, Bryce almost fired. Fuentes did not get the gun all the way up. It dropped and he dropped with it.

Bob Bryce waited. The other two men, stuck there with those useless scatterguns which could not reach as far as the lower end of town, were running sudden gushes of sweat. One of them called unsteadily. " It's all right, mister. It's all over. We ain't takin' it up."

Bryce was satisfied. " Shed the shotguns; leave the gunbelts up there too . . . Good. Now step ahead gents and lie belly-down in the dirt right beside your friend there. You heard what I said . . . Face down beside that friend of yours, arms out from the shoulders. And don't move. Don't even cough!"

The men obeyed, humiliated almost past endurance. Everyone around town was watching, from some private place of vantage. Fuentes and his corralyard hostlers had ruled Shepler's Spring and the countryside in all directions for hundreds of miles, ever since Fuentes had arrived here as station-master. His men, encouraged by the local fear of Fuentes, had swaggered their share. Now, they were lying in the manured roadway on their bellies, and Manuel was dead.

Bob Bryce turned as he lowered the carbine. " Blacksmith . . . you object?"

The unsmiling, whiskered face showed nothing when the reply came. "No objection, mister. I think it's been a long time coming. You won't get any arguments—not in town." He jerked his head. "This here is Simon Langley. He owns the saloon . . . Simon?"

"Good riddance," conceded Simon. "But mister, he's got those two you made lie down, and three more around the corralyard somewhere. You continue to stand like that, in the centre of the road and somebody's goin' to potshoot you."

Bryce ignored the warning, which made the blacksmith wag his head. Simon sat like a carving, watching without so much as moving a hand.

Bryce started forward, he had the cocked saddle-gun in both hands ready to swing and fire in an instant. But nothing happened. He got up to where the three men were lying in the sunbright roadway, went past to collect the weapons and pitch them towards the opposite side of the roadway, then he walked back, behind the prone men, and said, "Turn the Mex over."

Both the corralyard men sat up, slowly, looked back, looked down at Fuentes and rolled him. There was a small hole close to the centre of Fuentes's chest. He was dead. Bryce motioned, "Get up, you two." They obeyed, faces streaked with sweat and dirt. "You work for that Mex?" he asked, and when they both nodded without saying a word, Bryce gave them an order. "Go get your bedrolls, saddle up and ride out. Don't stop until you're out of the country, and don't come back. You understand?"

They nodded again, woodenly, then hesitated as though unwilling to enter the corralyard when their backs would be to Bryce. He jerked his head, they looked at one another, then finally walked away.

Bryce reached the same side of the roadway, stepped onto the plank-walk and strolled back southward as far as the shoeing shed where Simon Langley was slowly wagging his head, evidently in disbelief. From the corner of his mouth he softly spoke to the horseshoer. " I don't see how he got away with it."

The blacksmith said nothing. He watched Bob Bryce approach, let out a long breath and rose from the bench. " A dollar," he said to the sinewy stranger, as though being paid for shoeing the black horse was the only thing on his mind. " You shouldn't have turned those two loose. You got some fair odds against you. About five to one."

Bryce, with the unkempt old cottonwood trees protecting his back, leaned aside the carbine, dug out a silver cartwheel, passed it over and looked steadily at the smith. " Your name is Shepler?"

The smith nodded while pocketing the money.

" You're related to the folks who started this town?"

" Yes. It was my paw. He was a Kentuckian. Him and my maw are buried west of town in the burial plot." Henry Shepler turned his head. Three men were carrying Manuel Fuentes inside the corralyard. They did not even look southward. Shepler said, " Mister, I'll tell you again. Head out and ride fast."

Bob Bryce also turned, but he only caught a glimpse because those men up yonder were passing inside the gateway with Fuentes. "How long's he been riding roughshod down here, blacksmith?"

Shepler was slow to answer, which was his way in serious matters, so Simon Langley answered. "Several years. He replaced a man named Hank Evarts who used to be way-station boss here in Shepler's Spring. He worked for the company up north somewhere. A traveller once told me at my bar Fuentes came from up on the Colorado-Wyoming line. Mister, Henry just gave you good advice."

Bryce sighed. He had been getting this same warning often enough since his run-in with Manuel Fuentes. "When I'm ready," he told Langley, and went down into the shed to up-end his carbine and sink it back into the boot. Then he went out where his horse was tied, brought the animal round to the trough for it to tank up, and leaned upon the horse's back studying the empty, utterly silent roadway up through town.

If there were five men angered by the killing of Manuel Fuentes, they were being very circumspect about their desire for vengeance.

Langley trudged back on a diagonal course for his saloon, and Henry Shepler walked over to stand near the trough batting away agitated mud-daubers who had been disturbed by the drinking horse standing in the mud at the base of the old leaky trough, where the wasps hovered.

The horse swished his tail, raised his head, trickling

water while he glanced around, then he cleansed his mouth and dropped his head to sip a little more.

Bob Bryce gazed at Henry Shepler. " He broke a couple of ribs in the old man's dog."

Shepler said, " And for that you killed him?"

Bryce kept watching Shepler's impassive, rusty-bearded face. " No. For that I gave him a dose of his own medicine. I killed him, Mister Shepler, because that's the way he wanted it. Otherwise he wouldn't have been waiting out there for me with his two shot-gun friends. I couldn't have ridden out of here, and if I had, I'll tell you what I think; a couple of his friends were somewhere beyond town waiting for me. Other-wise, why didn't they come out shooting a few minutes ago? Because they're not in the corralyard, Mister Shepler. There was just one man up there, and he didn't have the guts."

Henry considered that suggestion. " Maybe," he con-ceded, grudgingly giving silent respect to the clear-eyed man leaning on the black horse. " And what do you figure to do? The longer you wait around, the surer they are to nail you."

Bob Bryce kept studying Henry Shepler. Eventually he said, " Why didn't someone do it before, if he was bullyin' folks?"

Henry's reply to that was forthright. " Because he was fast, and because he had those fellers working for him up there who did exactly what he told them to do —which means murder too, if that's what he told them to do."

Bob's horse raised his head, dripping water, tanked up now and waiting for whatever came next.

Bryce led the horse back to the shady side of the shed and re-tied him, then he went inside the shed and rolled a smoke. When Henry come in Bryce said, " Sorry to have to inconvenience you, blacksmith, but I'm not familiar with the country, and they could bushwhack me pretty easy. I'll wait here until dark."

3

" I'LL DRINK TO THIS FELLER!"

A large, slightly paunchy man named Mike Reader had owned the Shepler's Spring General Store for eighteen years, ever since he had bought it from the daughter of its founder. Back in those days there was still a tan-yard out back, not used very much but with the bad odour of all tan-yards.

Mike had discouraged the bringing in of hides. Undoubtedly that had been a big part of the previous owner's trade, but Mike did not have the stomach for it. He did not especially need the additional revenue. Shepler's Spring had not grown much in eighteen years, but the freight and stage traffic passing through certainly had grown.

Mike was a widower who lived well and comfortably in the back of his store. He had actually had little contact with Manuel Fuentes. He had known, of course, that Fuentes was a bully and a gunman, but, as he was telling Simon over the bar, every town had at least one like that, and ordinarily they were worse; they stole, and challenged people, and killed indiscriminately. Fuentes, at least, had killed no one around Shepler's Spring—that Mike Reader had heard of anyway.

Simon looked disapprovingly at the storekeeper, and at his left side, standing beside Reader, was Henry Shepler. Simon knew from Henry's expression he too did not agree with Reader, so Simon said, " Fuentes has kept folks from settlin' here, Mike. He's beat up a dozen fellers for no particular reason, he's brought in the scum of the territory to work as swampers in his corralyard, and . . ." Simon lowered his voice to a conspiratorial whisper, " . . . you say he's killed no one around here—well—what about those letters the Town Council gets every once in a while about missing people?"

Mike Reader reared back to look disgustedly at the barman. " There's not one darned breath of proof Fuentes had anything to do with those missing people, Simon. Someone is always turning up missing out here. Especially in summertime."

Henry Shepler broke in. " Mike—you favoured Manuel?"

That was going a little far, but Reader shrugged when he answered. " All I'm tryin' to say, Henry, is that killin' someone over an old dog who probably wouldn't have lasted another couple of years anyway . . ." He let it trail off while he stood looking at the blacksmith.

Henry said, " It wasn't over the dog," repeating what he had been told.

Mike Reader stiffened. " It wasn't? Fuentes is dead isn't he?"

" Yeah, he's dead. He got killed because he was out there in the middle of town with two of his swampers, all of them loaded for a killin' and it backfired on them. About the dog—the young feller knocked Manuel senseless for kickin' the old dog."

Simon, looking pleased, said, " Mike, Fuentes had three to one odds. That was his way. Only this time it didn't work. He's no loss. For one, I'm darned glad he's gone. You'd ought to be too."

Reader sighed, rolled up his eyes and shoved the beer glass forward for a re-fill. When Simon went up the bar with the empty glass in hand, Mike Reader turned and said, " Henry, don't get me wrong. I'm glad Fuentes is out of it. Personally, I never had trouble with him, but that was because I was right careful . . . I'm real glad Shepler can start breathin' again—but it just seemed to me, killin' someone because they kicked a dog . . ."

Henry waited until Simon returned and placed the refilled glass before Mike, then he said, " Bryce is the young feller's name. Bob Bryce. And he's settin' over in my shop waiting for dark."

Simon scowled. " I figured he'd left town long ago."

" No," stated the horseshoer. " He used his head. There was three of Manuel's men at the corralyard, which meant two more were somewhere else. Mister Bryce figured they were out yonder somewhere ready to bushwhack him. So he's goin' to wait until dark before heading out. Nothing wrong with that—except that if Manuel's men get organized and start trouble, it's not goin' to take them long to figure where Mister Bryce is setting."

Simon said, " You better get him out of there, Henry."
Shepler raised his bearded countenance. " How?"

Simon became busy with his sour old bar-rag, and
standing beside Henry, the storekeeper squinted into
his beer for a while. Eventually he parroted the barman. " If you don't get him out of there, Henry, and
Fuentes's men figure out he's waiting here in town,
and start something, it could be serious."

The blacksmith turned the same look on Reader.
" How, Mike?"

" Well, just walk down there and tell him."

Shepler continued to gaze at the storekeeper. " He
killed a man this afternoon, Mike. I should just walk
up and tell him to get out of my shed? Tell you what,
Mike, since it's your idea, *you* do it."

A lanky, rawboned older man with unkempt grey-
white hair stalked in from the roadway stuffing a soiled
cloth apron aside and into a trouser pocket as he ad-
vanced on the bar. His name was Amos Cody and it
was rumoured that he was related to Buffalo Bill Cody,
something which Amos neither confirmed nor denied,
he simply did not talk about it at all.

When he reached the bar he looked around and said,
" Too bad about Manuel Fuentes," and before he could
send Simon for a glass Henry Shepler glared and said,
" What's too bad about it?"

The big old rawboned saddlemaker smiled. " Too
bad it didn't happen three, four years ago. Simon, salt
a glass of beer for me, will you?"

They explained about Bob Bryce sitting over there

26

in the blacksmith shop. Amos was sympathetic. He kept bobbing his head at any rate, but once his beer with the shot of whiskey in it got back and he tasted it, he said, " I don't blame the young feller. Sure as hell they'll bushwhack him if they can." He drank deeper the second time, then leaned, gazing at the backwall feeling the wonderfully tingly and relaxing sensation moving throughout his aged and lanky carcass.

The other men leaned there saying nothing, but Mike Reader had a pained expression on his heavy face. " He rides in here, shoots someone, makes trouble for everyone, hangs around to make more trouble!"

The saddlemaker put down his mug and gazed at Reader. " He didn't make no trouble for me, Mike. What trouble, anyway? That son of a bitch Fuentes had had this town tucking its tail for five years." Amos lifted his mug again. " For one, I'll drink to this feller." He paused. " What's his name?"

Shepler said, " Bob Bryce," and watched old Amos Cody salute the name and drain his mug. He then set it down hard atop the bar and looked around with brighter eyes. Simon did not ask, he took the mug along the bar to re-fill it.

Mike Reader continued to look dour, but having been argued down, he was content to lean there in unhappy silence until Henry Shepler said, " Well, maybe we're worryin' too much. Maybe nothing'll happen." He raised his eyes in the direction of the back-bar clock as though estimating in his head how much time the town would have to wait out, until Bryce rode away.

27

Mike Reader left. A few minutes later old Hap Sunday came shuffling in from the back alley. He entered the bar-room by way of Langley's storeroom, blinked around, saw the hunched figures, and seemed hesitant until Henry saw him and said, " Hap, you want a drink?"

The old man shuffled forward, pleased to be noticed.

Simon wordlessly drew off a glass of beer and set it in front of the old man. When Henry fished out a coin Simon said, " Forget it."

Hap drank, savoured his beer, drank a little more and said, " I don't know why he kicked m'dog."

Henry stared into his glass and Amos asked for details. Hap gave them, then mumbled to himself and took his glass of beer to a chair, carrying it as though it were liquid gold. The saddlemaker looked from Henry to Simon.

" Is that true?"

Henry nodded. He had seen it happen. Simon hadn't so he said nothing.

Amos, big and rangy, rough and scarred, old and sinewy, said, " What was the dog doing?"

" Nothing," stated Henry Shepler. " Hap sat on that old bench in front of the way-station. Manuel came out, said something to Hap, and the old dog wasn't even lookin' at Manuel. He upped and gave him a hell of a kick."

" Hurt him?" asked the saddlemaker and got a sardonic glance from the horseshoer. "Yeah it hurt him. Bowled him over and he couldn't get up. Bryce went up there, knocked Manuel senseless and carried the old dog home for Hap."

Amos Cody thought it over, shoved his mug at Simon with a growl, and as the barman walked away Amos said, "The old dog's just about deaf, Henry."

"I know that."

"He didn't pee on the building or anything?"

"No. I was out front and saw it happen. The old dog didn't have any idea it was coming."

Old Amos waited. When his re-fill came back he tasted it, smacked his lips then said, "I think this stranger deserves a few friends."

Henry and Simon exchanged a glance then looked elsewhere.

Amos straightened up. "He's over at your shop, Henry?"

"Yes."

"I think I'll take him over some suds. Simon, fill a little pail for me."

Simon obeyed, Amos paid for the beer and turned back carrying the beer pail in one big old work-thickened hand. Simon waited until Amos was gone then rolled his eyes. "They'll see him take that beer over there."

Henry knew this. "Simon, I got to tell you something. That was a lousy thing for Fuentes to do."

"All right," agreed the saloon proprietor. "*I* know that. But Mike's partly right too, Henry. This isn't our fight. Over a damned dog."

Henry straightened up. "I explained that. It wasn't entirely over the dog. Manuel just made a mistake—

this time. He bearded a feller who was more than his match." Henry waited, then also said, "But even if it *had* been over the dog, it was still a lousy thing to do."

" Where are you going?"

" Over to the shop."

" You hadn't ought to. Sure as hell Fuentes's men are all in town by now, and they'll figure out where Bryce is."

Shepler gravely inclined his head, did not comment, and turned to depart.

Simon made an absent-minded swipe over his bartop with the smelly rag he had tucked in his apron-top, watched the doors swing to behind Shepler, and heaved a big, noisy sigh.

The afternoon stage came in early, sashayed wide in the roadway so as to make a neat entrance between the pole-gates of the corralyard, and Simon, who did not bother looking out the fly-specked front window went over to polish some glasses and get ready for the inevitable invasion of parched male customers.

It happened twice daily this time of year, and when full summer arrived, with more passengers using the stages, his trade increased proportionately to the rising summertime heat.

Today, with the sun canting away so that sooty shadows could form over on the opposite side of the road, he got just one stranger, a youngish man with hawkish features, bronzed from exposure to wind and sun, who came in beating off dust with his hat.

He was dressed better than most rangemen and had an

ivory butt on his sixgun, but Simon, who was a good judge of men, was sure this one was one of those itinerant rangeriders before the stranger reached the bar and smiled as he called for a beer.

Simon brought it back and asked if there were more passengers. The cowboy drank first, then answered. " Yeah. A woman." That was all he volunteered as he stepped back to roll a smoke to go with his beer. Simon watched, decided this one had to be a tophand—he had that calm air of complete self-confidence—and when the stranger had lighted up Simon asked the condition of the roadway, which was usually the way these conversations got started.

The stranger smiled easily. He seemed to be an amiable, good-natured man. " Like straddling a washboard the full distance from Catlin."

That established the direction from which the hawkish-looking rangeman had come. Simon pinned it down with a question. " All the way from Utah ?"

The cowboy looked thoughtfully at Simon. "Yeah. All the way from Utah." He finished the beer and shoved the glass away as he smoked and leaned in solid comfort. " Quiet town," he said.

Simon considered that. " Seems like it anyway," he muttered.

Old Hap shuffled over to place his empty glass atop the bar and said, " I don't want Colonel to die, Simon."

The cowboy turned, took Hap's measure in a glance, and listened when Simon said, " Aw, he won't die, Hap. He'll be all right."

31

" But there wasn't no call to kick him," Hap said, looking straight at Simon from watery old sunken eyes. " You know he's always been a good dog, Simon. He don't hear good any more, but he don't bite and if Manuel had give us a chance we'd have gone away."

The cowboy dropped his smoke and stepped on it, then put a quizzical look on old Hap. " Someone hurt your dog, oldtimer?"

Hap turned. " Kicked him and he was bleedin' at the mouth and couldn't get up. I think Colonel will die, mister."

Simon swiped the bartop vigorously, considered Hap's empty glass and said, " You want a re-fill, Hap?"

The old man looked at the glass. " Can't," he muttered.

The hawk-faced man said, " Sure you can. Fill it up, bartender. Tell me about the dog, oldtimer."

Simon heard Hap's monotone as he went up the bar to lever beer back into the sticky glass again. Now, he was almost ready to agree with Mike Reader. This thing was beginning to look as though it might get out of hand. Maybe, if old Hap was a little drunk he'd go on home.

Simon poured a few drops of ' salt ' into the glass along with the beer and took it back. Hap had finished explaining about the incident over in front of the way-station and the rangeman gave Simon a sharp glance when the barman returned. He said, " Who the hell is this Fuentes?"

Simon's answer was frank. " Who *was* he. This feller

who helped Hap and his old dog, killed him."

The cowboy's level, pale eyes widened slightly, so Simon told him the rest of the story. When he finished the rangeman retrieved his glass and shoved it over. As Simon reached for it the stranger said, "Do you have a marshal in town?"

They hadn't had a lawman in Shepler's Spring since anyone could remember. "No sir. We aren't that big. Besides, there's never any trouble here."

The stranger watched Simon hike up to re-fill his glass. He kept watching Simon, even when old Hap took his drink and shuffled back to his chair. Standing for any length of time made his legs, his hips and back ache. He had been hurt a lot of times in his life on bucking horses, in stampedes, being run down and gored by bull buffaloes, and with several rifle balls. Those things had not troubled him much forty years earlier, but they troubled him now.

When Simon returned the cowboy had a question for him. "What do you folks figure to do?"

Simon shrugged and borrowed something from Henry. "Nothing. Wait until dark and hope the feller gets away from here without any more trouble." Simon smiled.

The rangerider picked up his glass, drank slowly, put it down and studied Simon. "Nice town you got here," he said, and it could have been sarcasm but Simon wasn't sure, so all he said was, "Mister, we been putting up with Fuentes a long while."

The cowboy's nice smile came up. "You fellers must

thrive on a diet of crow, eh?"

Simon reddened a little. "Mister, we been gettin' along. I guess most places they got someone like Fuentes. It's sure as hell not a perfect world, is it?"

The cowboy's smile widened. "So sir, bartender, it sure as hell isn't. This feller—he's over at the black-smith's shop? By any chance do you know his name?"

"Bryce, they tell me. Bob Bryce."

The man with the ivory-handled sixgun did not bat an eye. He kept looking directly at Simon for a long while, then grunted, drank more beer and said, "You don't say. Bob Bryce." Then he shoved the half-empty glass away, dropped a silver coin atop the bar and walked out.

4

THE PROBLEM

Simon heard the gunshot in total astonishment. The good-natured tophand had just left his saloon. Old Hap jumped as though he had been shot, and that confused Simon even more.

He came from behind the bar, apron flapping, and went to the front window, prudently standing a little to one side.

The rangeman with the ivory-handled gun was down just beyond the plank-walk, slowly and clumsily trying to lever himself up in the roadway dirt.

As far as Simon could see there was no one in sight. Hap came unsteadily over to crane out the window. He grunted and muttered to himself at sight of the weakly moving man in the roadway.

Simon rolled and tucked his apron. He had no wish at all to go out there, but it did not appear anyone else was going to and clearly that cowboy was unable to get up by himself. As he stepped around Hap he said, " Gawddammit," and headed for the door. Old Hap looked around. " What was that, Simon? What'd you say?"

Simon turned at the doorway. " Hap, you better go

home. Go out the back way."

"But I haven't finished my drink yet, Simon."

The barman hesitated a moment regarding the old man, then turned and pushed out into the waning sunlight.

The shot man had got into a sitting sprawl, his eyes were wide with shock, his movements were slow and poorly coordinated. Simon knew nothing about wounded men but instinct told him the rangerider had been hard hit. He stepped off the plank-walk sweeping the yonder buildings and the roadway with a swift look, saw no one until he got out where he knelt beside the shot man, then someone stepped forth from Henry's shop southward and upon the opposite side of the roadway. It was the saddlemaker, his shock of unkempt grey-white hair pointing in all directions. He stood like a pillar of rock watching Simon get a good grip on the stranger, and hoist him by sheer strength into a standing-leaning posture, encircle the man's middle and start toward the swinging doors with him. Then Amos turned, called to Henry, and they both stood watching as Simon struggled unsteadily until he got the rangeman inside where old Hap, still by the window, stood with his mouth open, watching.

Like most oldtime frontiersmen with a very limited knowledge of cures and medicines, Hap shuffled over to the chair where Simon eased the wounded man down, and said, " Get some whiskey down him, Simon."

It probably was good advice, but Simon stood up looking at warm blood on his hands, then leaned for a closer inspection. The stranger had been shot along the right side. His shirt was torn and bloody. There was a gushing long gash of ragged flesh. But as well as Simon could tell now, the bullet had not entered the man's body although it had ploughed a deep groove along the rib-cage and Simon could see wet white bone where the blood was running.

He hastened behind the bar, got several clean bar-rags and hastened back, ripped the shirt away and applied a bandage to stop the bleeding. The rangeman was breathing shallowly with his eyes closed and his ruddy complexion gone white and slack.

Amos and Henry came in from the back-alley, stared, then crossed over with long strides. Both of them were more experienced at this sort of thing than Simon was. They took over with nothing more than grunts, and when Hap repeated his earlier suggestion Henry looked up. "Whiskey, Simon."

Amos worked and shook his head at the same time. When Simon returned to hand the bottle to Henry, Amos said, "Who shot him?"

Simon had no idea. "I heard the noise was all. When I got to the window he was down out there. Hell, he'd just left my bar."

"Who is he?" Henry asked, balancing the wounded man's head so he could pour down the whiskey.

"All I know, Henry, is that he came in on the late-day stage. He had a drink and we talked a little. That's everything I know."

Amos dried blood off his hands on his beeswax-stiff

harness-maker's apron, stood up to examine critically the thick, rough bandage they had wrapped completely around the man's upper body, then held out his hand. Henry put the whiskey bottle in it. Amos took two big swallows, saw Simon watching, and as he handed over the bottle he said, " I owe you two bits." Then he turned, eyed Hap, who was beginning to weave a little, and kicked a chair around for the old man, and gently pushed him down on it. Then he said, " Henry, does this feller look a little like Bryce to you?"

The blacksmith's normally expressionless features creased into a mild frown. " You think that was it?"

Amos belched first, then said, " What else would it be? He just come into town on the late-day coach, had a drink, walked out of the saloon, and some son of a bitch shot him."

Shepler was not ready for this just yet, so he said, " Simon, you still got that old army cot in the store-room?"

" Yes. He's heavy as hell. It'll take all three of us to get him in there."

Simon was correct, only now the man with the ivory-stocked sixgun was almost completely inert. He could no longer make his legs obey so they had to practically carry him to the storeroom.

They removed his boots and hat, his gun and shell-belt, placed him out full length and Simon went in search of some old army blankets to cover him with. Finally, now, Henry was willing to discuss abstractions as he stood impassively eyeing the barely-conscious stranger.

"Suppose he dies, Amos?"

The saddlemaker, a pragmatic man who had lived long enough to have seen death in many forms, stood gazing at the stranger. "Maybe he's got some identification on him so's we can notify his family. If he's got one." Then Amos said, "But hell, he's not goin' to die. I've seen those rib wounds before. If he don't get the gangrene or some kind of bad infection he'll make it. Look at him, healthy as a stud-horse, Henry."

Simon brought the blankets, covered the semi-conscious man then stepped back frowning. He was not happy over having a wounded man in his storeroom. "What he needs is a doctor, Henry, and someone who can look after him for a week or two." Simon let go a rattling big sigh. "What in the hell's going on in town? We never had anything like this before."

Neither of the other men answered. They had done all they knew to do. From here on, it seemed it would have to be up to the wounded man himself, and, as Amos had noted, he looked strong and healthy.

They went back out front. Old Hap was gone but they did not notice this as they trooped to the bar. Simon, who rarely drank, filled three shot-glasses and dropped his jolt straight down, then made a face.

Henry toyed with his glass, his thoughts not on drinking. "All right," he announced. "Now we got to *do* something, Simon, didn't you see anyone after you went outside?"

"Not a soul."

" Well, *someone* shot that man. We got to do something about this."

Amos downed his jolt without batting an eye. " If it was Manuel's hostlers at the corralyard, and they mistook this stranger for Bryce, we got trouble on our hands."

" We'll have more trouble," stated the blacksmith, " if we don't get this straightened out. Maybe they'll shoot someone else."

Mike Reader came in from the roadway acting slightly breathless. He had seen the downed man out front of the saloon. They told him what they knew, which was not much more than he had already surmised. Then they told him what they had just been discussing, and at once the storekeeper began bridling. " Wait," he cautioned. " Just let's set back and wait. It'll be dark in another couple of hours and Bryce can make a run for it. But mainly, he can get the hell out of town, and if they go after him, they'll be out of town too."

Henry looked dourly around. " One thing wrong with that, Mike. Even if they get Bryce beyond town, or if he gets clear and they don't get him, we still got this other feller."

" He'll mend won't he? All right, it was an accidental shooting. He just happened to walk into someone else's bullet. It's too bad but those things got a way of happening. And when he can ride again, we can maybe take up a collection and buy him a seat on the stage, and get him out of here too. I tell you fellers, the wisest thing for us to do is—nothing. Just set back and let it blow itself out."

Henry was not through. " Mike, Bryce and this other feller aren't all of it. Fuentes may be gone, but the feller who just shot the stranger, and those other renegades across at the corralyard, are still here. You think, if they get Bryce, they're goin' to turn into decent citizens all of a sudden?"

Reader stared at the horseshoer. " What you got in mind? Henry, I'm not goin' to be part of a posse, if that's what you're driving at."

Shepler said no more. He finally drank his whiskey and was putting down the glass when Simon spoke from the other side of the bar.

" I think Henry's right, Mike. Those five men over across the road aren't likely to just ride out because Manuel's dead . . . Have you seen anyone leavin' town?"

Reader hadn't. " No, but give them time."

Henry snorted. " Bryce told two of 'em to leave and they haven't done it. I don't figure they'll go. I also think that Fuentes had a reason for holding them in check. He had the stage and freight franchise here in town. But those renegades got nothing to make them hold off. Mike, if they take a notion to raid town your store's going to be first."

Reader looked disgusted. " You fellers are imagining things," he exclaimed, but when the other three stood there gazing at him in silence, he turned to the bar and asked Simon for a drink.

Henry turned his sticky glass back and forth in its

little wet ring atop the bar. After a while he offered a suggestion. "Let's talk all this out with Bryce."

No one dissented, not even Mike Reader who downed his shot of whiskey and blinked his eyes very rapidly afterwards. He was not much of a drinker.

Simon went back to the storeroom to look in on the wounded man. When he returned he was solemn. "He'd have to look better just to die," Simon reported.

Amos was knowledgeable. "Shock. A bullet'll do that to you. Jolts hell out of your system. He's not going to die . . . All right, let's go over and talk to Bryce."

But they did not use the front door, and out in the back-alley they kept looking sharply around as they walked southward, down where they had to reach the roadway. The town was as quiet as a tomb. Reader shook his head. "What are they doin' up there at the corralyard, for gosh sakes."

Henry said, "Drinkin' Manuel's wine. Come along."

Nothing happened as they crossed the road, but each one of them walked stiffly and cagily, as though they expected something to happen.

Bryce had seen them, was watching as they came over to the shoeing shed, and pitched his smoked-down cigarette into the cooling forge as he waited.

He had reloaded the saddlegun, had put his horse inside where it had protection in case someone decided to set him afoot in this village, and when the townsmen walked in he nodded and stood waiting. They had entered the shop as though they were a delegation, so clearly they had something to say.

42

Henry acted as spokesman. He related what had happened to the stranger, calling it a case of mistaken identity, which Bob Bryce was willing to believe. Henry then said it was the opinion of the townsmen that whether he left town after dark or not, Shepler's Spring was still going to be saddled with those five gunmen up at the corralyard.

Bryce's answer to that was perhaps predictable. "Gents, you've lived with those men for several years, and I'm sure nowhere close to bein' a lawman. It's up to you whatever you decide to do."

Amos was exasperated by this. " Mister, we maybe could have lived with Manuel for another five years, but *you* shot the son of a bitch, we didn't. This may not be your town, but you sure as hell brought this mess on. All we'd like is for you to lend us a hand while we try and root those fellers out, up there, and run them the hell out of town."

Bob Bryce slowly smiled at Amos. " That's all? Tell me something : Are any of you good with guns?"

Amos spluttered. " Well, thirty, forty years back I held my own."

Henry knew what the answer to that was going to be, so he spoke before Bryce could say anything, using a quieter tone than the harness-maker had used. " Mister Bryce, you're not goin' out of here scot-free. By now those fellers all know what you look like. They shot a man who looks a little like you. They're waitin' for dark too. Then they're comin' after you. I see this like something we're *all* on. If you try to escape alone, mister,

I just don't think you've got the chance of a snowball in hell."

Bryce looked at Henry for a long while, then said, " Four against five, blacksmith?"

" That beats hell out of five to one, Mister Bryce."

The rangeman slowly smiled at Henry. " You missed your trade, blacksmith. You should have travelled with one of those medicine shows. All right. I guess you got it figured about right. Now tell me the rest of it, since you gents have been figuring things out. How the hell do we smoke them out of that corralyard into the open?"

No one answered because no one had any idea how that was to be accomplished.

5

SOMETHING NEW

Henry Shepler and Mike Reader had always done the most business with Manuel Fuentes. The up-shot of the lengthy discussion in the shoeing shed was that those two should go up to the corralyard and palaver with the hostlers; try and acquire some idea of what those men had in mind and what they intended to do.

Henry may have been an individual of little or no imagination, because it did not particularly trouble him, thinking about walking in up there, but Mike Reader was negative in everything he said about being part of a team of pow-wowers, and no one expected Mike to act any differently.

They left Simon in the shed with Bob Bryce and walked northward in the weakening daylight with its soft hues of copper and dusty russet. Two women were standing in the cafe window opposite, one of them a stranger to both Henry Shepler and Michael Reader. The other woman was Rosie O'Leary who owned the cafe.

She was the greying widow of a man who had once driven for the Nevada Stage & Cartage Company. He had been killed on the eastern desert in a runaway brought about by some highwaymen firing guns as they ran alongside.

Mike knew Rosie as well as anyone around town did, and seeing her across the road with that other, larger and more shapely woman, made him straighten slightly as he marched along.

Henry said, " I hope to hell they haven't been drinkin' *too* much"

They hadn't. But the smell of liquor was on the breath of the hatchet-faced, unshaven man who let them walk into the yard before speaking from behind them as he turned an uncocked scattergun in their direction.

They halted. The hostler came around to face them, his close-set tawny eyes full of malice. Two additional men came out of the way-station by a corralyard doorway. They looked, then sauntered over. Henry knew them all, not by name, by their faces.

He said, " Where's Halder?"

The narrow-faced man snarled back. " What do you want him for? We been watchin' you fellers sneakin' around town."

Pete Halder had been corralyard boss under Manuel Fuentes. Henry Shepler was assuming Halder was now in charge. " We want to talk to him," he said frankly. " Somebody shot a feller a while ago, and we want to get all this settled and over with."

A large, swarthy man emerged from the corralyard bunkhouse along the back wall, hitched at a gunbelt and sauntered forward with an air of command. He was chewing tobacco. When he could recognize the black-

46

smith and the storekeeper past the backs of his fellow hostlers, he smiled and called over to them. "Henry— Mike . . ." Then he shouldered past to show the only expression lacking malevolence. "You fellers got a problem?" he asked, acting relaxed and confident.

One of the other men repeated what Henry had said, and swarthy, burly Pete Halder nodded indifferently. "Yeah, that stranger got shot. But he warn't the right man, was he? We didn't see he was packing an ivory-handled Colt until he went down. I guess it was a mistake, Henry. Too bad, eh?"

Shepler's normally expressionless face showed nothing when next he spoke. "Pete, the man who shot that feller had better leave town."

Halder's bushy dark brows climbed. "Why, Henry? You got no constable in town."

The corralyard boss was clearly playing a game. Henry seemed to understand this. "We can get a law-man in here, Pete."

Halder looked mocking. "Sure you can. In a week. By then you'll need him a damned sight more than you do right now, Henry. But we're reasonable fellers. We don't aim to make trouble." Halder's black eyes lost their mocking humour now. "Where is that son of a bitch who shot Manuel? We made our decision, Henry. You hand him over—or we burn your damned two-bit town to the ground, with you fellers in the middle of it."

Mike Reader blanched. "We didn't know he was going to fight Manuel. We didn't even know he was in town, until the fight happened, Pete."

47

One of those other men snorted. "Henry knew, Mister Reader. He was shoein' that feller's horse."

Halder was not diverted. He said, "Hand him over, and things'll be back to normal. Protect him, and you'll regret it the rest of your damned lives."

Henry Shepler stood looking directly at Halder. They could prolong this, make an argument out of it, make threats and promises and nothing would be changed. He said, "Pete, that was a fair fight. More than fair. Manuel had two men out there with him. It's unfortunate that it happened, but it was a fair fight."

Halder did not dispute this. "We want that feller, Henry, and that's all there is to it. And we don't figure to horse around here forever until we get him." Halder pointed out through the gateway to the saloon across the road. "We're goin' to torch that place tonight to show you we mean business. If you don't hand him over after that, Henry, the whole damned town goes up." Halder let his arm drop back to his side. "Is that all you came up here to say?"

Mike Reader spoke out. "Burning the town won't bring Manuel back. All that will do is get you boys on a wanted list."

Halder smiled without a shred of humour. "Mister Reader, we're already on a wanted list. Every one of us. Manuel never told you that, did he?" In the face of Reader's expression of dread, Pete Halder faced Henry Shepler again. "You goin' to hand him over?"

Henry lied without blinking. "Tell us where he is, Pete, and we'll go get him. We've been at Simon's place most of the afternoon. Maybe he left town during that time."

The hostlers stared steadily at Henry, possibly trying to decide if he was telling the truth, and it was distinctly in Shepler's favour, for once, that he was a man of very little facial expression.

Halder finally said, " Henry, you boys better find that son of a bitch."

There was no way to mistake the threat in those words. Henry flung his arms wide. " How, for Chris' sake? It's dark, and he might have ridden off in any direction."

" Just find him," stated the corralyard boss, hooking thumbs in his shellbelt, and when Henry started to protest again Pete Halder cut across with the only concession he would make. " All right. You got all night."

" In the dark?" exclaimed Shepler.

" Yeah, in the damned dark. Henry, we don't care how you do it, but you got to deliver him to us, alive, by ten o'clock in the morning." At Shepler's stare, the swarthy man also said, " Hell, you can mount six or eight fellers from here in town. They can scatter in all directions. One of them is bound to be on the right track, and see that feller come daylight."

" Pete, that feller's got about a three-hour head start," Henry exclaimed.

Halder conceded that. " Likely he has. Let me tell you something. Both of you. My friends here probably will give me hell for makin' this trade with you. They don't care if we get that feller or not. They like the

49

idea of ransackin' the town better'n hauling some killer up by the throat to a corral post."

Henry abandoned his role of protest and glanced at Reader who was looking stricken. "All right. We'll do our damndest," Henry muttered. "But there's a chance whoever finds him won't be able to get back by ten o'clock."

Halder smiled in silence. So did the men standing there with him. They clearly hoped the killer of Manuel Fuentes could not be produced before the time limit expired, so they could then ransack Shepler's Spring.

As Henry and Mike turned to depart Pete Halder said, "If you try and send out for the law, gents, it won't help you at all. So far we haven't done a damned thing you can prove against us. And if the law comes in here, it better be a big posse, and even then we'll just ride off and wait until the law leaves, then we'll come back, and not just burn your lousy town that time."

Henry walked back through the gate with Mike at his side. As they swung southward in the direction of the shoeing shop, someone burst out laughing back in the corralyard. This man was joined by other men, all laughing.

Reader did not say a word until they were back inside the blacksmith shop, then he started to blame Bob Bryce for everything, but Henry cut him off with a snarl. In the blacksmith's view, they could not afford to alienate anyone.

He related quietly everything which had been said

in the corralyard. Bryce and Amos and Simon Langley listened solemn-faced, then Amos scratched his head, spat, and said, " It could be a hell of a lot worse, gents." The other men stared. " They could have fired the town tonight. This way at least we got a little time."

" And what happens in the morning," asked Mike Reader in a bitter voice, " when they don't get Bryce?"

Amos looked wolfishly at the storekeeper. " Maybe they won't want him by then, Mike. We got all night to skulk up there, get into position and drop those bastards like flies."

Simon looked pained. " How you goin' to see 'em to drop them, Amos?"

Before the saddlemaker could reply Bob Bryce spoke. " We don't have to see them. We don't have to shoot them either, but if we can get up there, get on all sides of that corralyard, we can sure as hell make it hard for any of them to get *out*. They can't fire the town unless they can get across the road to do it."

This fresh suggestion occupied all their minds for a while. Henry went over to turn down the smoking wick of the shop lantern which had been lighted during his absence. The smoking diminished, but so also did the light. They looked like troubled phantoms in the gloomy, sooty old shoeing shed. When he turned back he said, " Mike, I been telling you for a couple of years we need a town marshal."

Reader flung out his arms. " All right, we'll hire one. But what good will that do us now? Not a damned bit!"

Bryce rolled and lit a smoke. His manner was detached as he studied his companions. He was not as tense and anxious as they were, with good reason; he did not own a store in Shepler's Spring where everything had been built of wood.

Amos, his ebullient spirit undaunted, his keenness undiminished, said, " We better get our carbines, gents, and meet back here." Amos looked at Bob Bryce. " You're provin' to be a friend of the town, mister. I for one sure appreciate that," then Amos looked straight at Mike Reader.

The storekeeper was still of two minds, but if anything could have influenced him it was Pete Halder's remark about burning the town. The largest building belonged to Mike Reader, and it was chock-full of saleable merchandise.

They left the shop by the alley exit, which may have helped some, but with daylight fast fading they probably did not have to be that cautious.

Normally, they would have gone separately to the cafe for supper this hour of the day. Now, none of them seemed to be particularly hungry, but Simon mentioned the wounded stranger in his storeroom, so Henry went to the back door of the cafe for some broth, when they had all got across the road, then took the pitcher with him to the rear door of the saloon.

Simon was already inside. He left Henry at the storeroom door to go on through to the bar-room. There were no customers, but Simon did not ordinarily leave his saloon unattended for any length of time, and that had been worrying him for the past hour or so.

While he was out front Henry entered the storeroom, groped for a lamp and lighted it, set the pitcher down and took the lamp to a crate near the cot. The stranger opened his eyes, rolled them until he had Henry in full sight, then closed them again. He was conscious but weak. Most of the shock had passed, but he did not respond when Henry told him about the broth and leaned to raise the stranger so he could drink.

The man swallowed with an effort. Henry got all the broth down him, then pulled up a crate and sat on it at the bedside. He asked the stranger how he felt and got no answer. He told the stranger the extent of his injury, and as he did so he looked closely at the man. He seemed to have either fainted or to have gone to sleep. Henry leaned and gently touched him. The stranger did not respond so Henry leaned back worrying. It occurred to him that the stranger was perhaps bordering on consciousness, and that could be a favourable sign.

He leaned, felt in the man's shirt pocket for something to identify the man with, and pulled out a small steel circlet with a star in the centre of it. The words Deputy United States Marshal were inscribed on the steel circlet around the star.

Henry stared, turned the badge over, turned it back, then raised his eyes to the bronzed, slack face in front of him. He palmed the badge and used both hands to grope through other pockets until he came up with a folded piece of paper.

Suspecting it was a letter, perhaps with a name on it, he leaned toward the lamp, unfolded the paper and got his second surprise. It was a warrant for the arrest of a fugitive named Robert Bruce Bryce.

Someone's hard boot-steps coming from the direction of the bar-room galvanized Henry Shepler. There was no time to return the badge and warrant to the unconscious man's pocket, so he jammed the articles into his own shirt pocket, then looked around as Simon Langley entered.

Simon scarcely more than glanced at Henry as he stepped over and looked at the stranger on the cot. "Did you get the broth down him?" he asked, and when Henry nodded Simon leaned to look closer. "Is he unconscious again?" Again Henry nodded.

"He sort of drifts back and forth." Henry touched the bandage. "We better change this and see if the wound's still bleeding."

It was not bleeding but it was a gory, wet sight, and now there was bluish swelling where they had pulled the ragged edges together. Simon swallowed, hard, then went after fresh clean bandages. During his absence Henry sat there looking at the stranger. Finally, he wagged his head. But when Simon returned Henry did not mention the warrant, the identity of the man it had been issued for, nor the badge. He silently worked with Simon re-bandaging the injured lawman.

When they were finished Simon blew down the lamp chimney, picked up the emptied pitcher and unconsciously tiptoed out of the room.

Henry went out front to the bar, poured himself a drink behind the bar and when Simon came along Henry handed him a silver coin, then wordlessly went around in front and leaned there staring at the back-bar shelves, saying nothing.

Simon cut across the horseshoer's private thoughts. " You got a carbine?"

Henry roused himself and shook his head. Simon reached under the bar and placed a carbine in front of the blacksmith. He had a second carbine leaning behind the bar, and as a final thought, he also brought forth a sawed-off shotgun, not the kind of weapon a man would choose for what they had in mind tonight but Henry said nothing discouraging.

They each had another drink, then went back out into the rear alley through the darkened saloon.

6

THE NIGHT

Bob Bryce had evidently been scouting up the back alley because by the time they all met again he told them he thought what had to be accomplished was to surround the corralyard from in front, from the direction of the main roadway because that was how they would leave if they decided to go ahead and fire the town without waiting until morning to see whether Fuentes's killer was produced or not.

He thought three of them ought to block access to the rest of the town from in front, which would leave the rear alley behind the corralyard, and the two other directions, north and south, to be watched by the remaining two men.

No one found fault with any of this, but Mike Reader said he wanted to be one of the men in front. He did not explain his reason, but he did not have to. His store was in front; southward a short distance, but still in front, upon the opposite side of the road from the corralyard, and evidently reluctant Mike Reader was no longer lukewarm to opposing Fuentes's renegades. Amos seemed amused by this. He leaned to tell Henry Shepler in a low voice in his opinion the best heroes rarely were motivated by anything more exalted than personal selfishness and private interest.

Bob Bryce assumed command. None of the others noticed, in particular, or made an issue of it. They were united in their purpose and that alone seemed to matter. Nevertheless Henry Shepler, who was never needlessly talkative, seemed a little more reticent with Bryce than he had been. No one noticed that either as the men stood for a moment looking at one another. Up to this point they had conferred; there was no danger in that, but from this point on there *was* danger. There was also the matter of the unknown. So far, except for shooting the stranger with the ivory-butted sixgun, Fuentes's corralyard renegades had remained inside their palisaded compound. That would change, at least their dormancy would change, the moment they discovered they were being stalked by townsmen.

Amos finally said, " Well; it'd sure help if a man could see in the dark, but I guess that works both ways. *They* can't see no better'n we can. Let's get on with it."

Henry, Simon and Mike slipped out front to blend with night shadows while Bob Bryce and Amos went out into the alley behind the shop.

There were stars, a horde of them, but the moon was no more than a curved, sharp little scimitar of light. Visibility was limited, but protective cover was good both out front and in the west-side alley.

Amos watched Bryce. The younger man moved from shack to shed to outbuilding with the sureness of some-one who may have done something like this before. Or else had a natural talent for it, which was what Amos Cody thought. If Henry had been back there he would have had a different opinion.

The corralyard had six-foot logs implanted in the ground completely around the interior compound. Unless a man was tall, or found something to stand upon, he could not see over into the yard, but, as Bob Bryce said when he and Amos huddled within view of the back wall of the corralyard, it would be a lot easier for the men *inside* to keep watch, than it would be for the men *outside*.

Amos leaned to squint along the skyline, but if there was a sentry over there he was not visible. Bryce was not satisfied with that.

" He's there. They're not just standing around, in there."

He increased his caution, which annoyed the harness-maker a little, even though he went along with it, and when they were directly behind the log wall, Bob Bryce reached, brushed Amos's arm, and pointed.

The faint glow of a cigarette showed, sometimes bright, sometimes dull as the smoker enjoyed his quirley. But they could not make out the man himself, so they ducked around a house across the alley, kept a cow-shed between themselves and the cigarette-smoker until they could get directly opposite him, and entered the old shed to slip along to the warped alley-way siding to peer out.

They saw the man. He was leaning on the posts, evidently standing on something in order to be that

58

high above the logs. But there was little showing except his head and shoulders. There was no sign of a weapon, the man had his floppy old hat shoved back; he was leaning indolently, his attitude even in that feeble, ghostly light, one of boredom.

Amos put his head close. "That's a feller called Hammer. I don't know whether that's his name or just what he's called, but I know him. He drinks a lot."

Bryce stood motionless in the smelly old cow-shed watching the sentinel. Right now, it looked to be a Mexican stand-off; the men inside the yard were watching and marking time, and the men outside were supposed to be doing the same thing. Bryce's disadvantage was that he knew none of those men and could only guess about them, so he leaned to speak to Cody.

"You reckon they'll stay in there and wait for morning?"

Amos thought, then answered tartly. "If Manuel was alive I'd say no—they wouldn't wait. But with Manuel gone, damned if I know what they might do. The boss of the yard is a big half-Mex named Pete Halder. He's nobody's fool. I don't know what he might do, but I *do* know if he comes at you, don't wait before you pull the trigger."

Outside the cow-shed a dog came sniffing behind the hiding men, then growled when he detected their scent inside. Amos turned, swore in a whisper, then felt in the darkness for a stone. What he found was a bone-dry cow chip. He stepped back and pitched it. The dog gave a jump and lit running. He sped northward toward the adjoining yard, then halted well beyond range and barked furiously.

Bryce watched the sentry across the alley. The man doused his smoke, straightened up a little and turned to peer off in the direction of the excited dog.

A second head appeared over there beside the sentry's head and shoulders. Bryce asked who the second renegade was and Amos shook his head. He could not make the man out well enough to name him.

They talked quietly, watching northward where the dog was beginning to get over his fright, then the second sentry said, " Probably a skunk or a 'coon after someone's hen-roost," words which carried perfectly to Bryce and Cody.

The sentry had lost interest as the dog's racket diminished. The dog was leaving, going northward evidently, from his sounds, and eventually he stopped barking altogether. That moment the watchers heard the sentry say : " They ain't goin' to do anything."

The second man had a deep, rumbling voice which lent resonance to his words when he answered. " That's what Pete says; they're a bunch of gawddamned storekeepers." The deep voice echoed scorn. " But personally, I don't think Pete should have given them the time to find that bastard who shot Manuel. We could've raided the town this afternoon and have been thirty miles away by now. . . . Pete's playing some kind of damned game; he's makin' 'em sweat. Maybe *he* likes somethin' like this, but I don't."

The sentry thought briefly, then said, " Well hell,

we could slip out o' here and plunder that saloonman's cash-box, and do the same down at the general store. That son of a bitch does a good business; he's bound to have money over there."

The deep-voiced man disagreed. "Hammer, once Pete talked to 'em, they sure as hell ran back and hid all their money. That's what I meant when I said Pete hadn't ought to have been cute with 'em. I told him a few minutes ago, those bastards more'n likely took all their money and rode out of town."

Clearly, this suggestion upset the sentry because he said, "Gawddammit. What's the sense of us stayin' in here, then?"

The deep-voiced man offered a curt answer to that. "Tell Pete. You don't have to gripe to me." He got down from whatever they were standing on and evidently walked away because the sentry turned to watch, then slowly turned back, and now he leaned a Winchester in sight atop the posts while he dug around for his makings and started manufacturing another smoke. He was upset, that was clear even in the poor light the watchers had to try and benefit from as they studied him.

Bryce stepped back from the crack in the old warped wood where he had been looking and listening. He did not speak for a while, then he said, "If they're arguin' among themselves . . ." He faced Amos. "You know them better than I do," but the saddlemaker could offer little enlightenment.

"I don't know what they'll do. But it sounded like

that second feller was about ready to sneak out and rob Simon's saloon."

"How about Halder—will he hold still for that?"

Amos's answer was non-committal. "Your guess is as good as mine." Then he leaned to peer through the old boards again. While he was doing that someone made a grating sound across the alley, so Bob Bryce leaned to look.

Amos whispered, "The gate."

Bryce had not noticed the alley-exit, which was a section of those upright logs, and in the darkness did not look different from the rest of the log wall until a person made a minute study, then four heavy steel hinges were visible on each panel of the gateway.

Amos whispered tensely. "Someone's comin' out."

But that was a premature judgment. Someone was opening one side of the gate, but they only opened it a yard or so, and no one emerged.

The gate was left ajar like that. Bryce and Amos watched intently. Whether someone had intended to slip out or not, some noise around in front, in the direction of the main roadway, may have changed his mind. The gate remained ajar, though, as Bryce's attention was diverted to this second situation, which seemed to be agitation inside the corralyard, but across toward the front gateway.

Amos pulled back to cock an enquiring eye. Bryce, striving to discern what that noise was about, ignored the older man. If the forted-up hostlers had discovered that there were three townsmen out front covering the front of the yard, it would account for the brief sounds of abrupt agitation inside the yard. Bryce looked for the smoking sentry over there. He was still in place, but now his back was to the alley while he peered inside and toward the front of the yard.

Bryce waited, then leaned to say, " I think we can get inside, Amos."

The saddlemaker scowled in the darkness. " Yeah? Then what? Get shot all to hell?"

Bryce stepped around to the sagging old broken door in the side of their building for a clear view of the alley, the back-wall opposite, and that ajar gateway. Amos came over also to look, but his craggy features were set in an adamant expression. He had not thought much of Bryce's suggestion before, and he clearly still did not think much of it. He pointed. The sentry was turning back to watching the alley again. Whatever had caused the commotion inside, had ended. Now, the night was as silent again as it had been before.

That open gate intrigued Bob Bryce, a man of daring and innovation, but of the men he was with tonight only one, Henry Shepler, even suspected he might be skilled at this sort of thing, and Henry was out front with Mike Reader and Simon Langley.

Amos, a bold man all his life, had lived to his present age by also being prudent. All that ajar gate meant to him was odds of five to one, or perhaps five to two. He had not reached sixty by being reckless.

His pointing out that the sentry was watching again had been his mute way of conveying to his younger companion the dangers involved with trying to steal across the alley, or getting inside the corralyard.

Bryce turned back into the shed, finally, which made Amos heave a small sigh of relief. He returned to his spying place in the back-wall and turned only once more to look back, and that was when someone's doe-eyed, bony, rusty-coloured milk-cow came to the door of her shed and peered in. Amos turned back; at least the cow would not bark.

Bryce made a smoke and went closer to the front of the shed to smoke it. The houses scattered around Shepler's Spring were few and far between. They were also dark. Even the inhabited ones showed no signs of life. Perhaps the scattered few townsmen knew what was impending, and willingly retired early to avoid implication, although it was even more possible that they did not know, and had retired early because that was the local custom.

Bryce killed his smoke, returned where Amos was looking across the alley, and said, " Anything?"

Amos bobbed his head without taking his eye away from the spy-hole. "Yeah. They're up to something along the back wall."

Bryce, with fresh interest, stepped back to the place where he had formerly spied, and looked out. The gate was still ajar, but now there was something occurring over there, stealthily, it seemed, and surreptitiously.

Amos, who had been looking and listening longer, thought he had heard a horse over there. " Maybe someone wants out," he speculated, " or they're sending someone away—for some darned reason."

Bryce returned to the side door of the shed where the view was better, and listened. There was indeed something going on behind the ajar gate. The sentry was now looking back down into the yard. Amos saw a swift shadow moving along the side of the shed and in surprise reached for his Winchester. Then he froze. It was Bryce taking advantage of the sentry's diverted interest to steal away from the cow-shed across an intervening open space to a hen-house which was almost directly opposite the palisade gateway. Amos swore to himself. There was no way for Bryce to return to the cow-shed if the sentry turned back, facing the alley and all the open areas around it.

Inside the back wall of the corralyard a shod hoof struck stone. Amos heard it very clearly. He had heard the same sound earlier. Bryce also had to have heard it and that worried Amos even more.

A man led a saddled horse out into the alley, stood briefly looking in all directions, then started across the alley westerly, leading his horse. Amos, puzzled and worried, watched the sentry. The man watched, but neither waved nor called to the man with the saddle-horse.

Amos saw the horseman pass from sight down the north side of the hen-house where he had last seen Bob Bryce, and held his breath expecting thunderous gun-shots. None came, the man leading the horse reappeared west of the hen-house, then he turned with the horse between him and the sentry atop the corralyard fence and walked in the direction of the cow-shed. Amos picked up his carbine. Whoever the man was with the horse, he had come from the corralyard which meant he was one of Fuentes's men, and right now Amos was perfectly willing to take a captive—if he could.

Evidently the man with the horse was leading his animal so as to be practically silent until he was far enough away to get astride.

Amos moved soundlessly to the cow-shed door through which Bryce had vanished, looked, saw the man leading the horse, guessed about where he might pass—around in front of the shed to the west where that disinterested milk-cow was still standing—and slipped over there. He would be beyond the sight of the corralyard sentry with the shed between them. It looked as though he could capture the horseman without much danger.

The horse looked black in the darkness. He was actually a chestnut sorrel. The man walking inches ahead leading the animal by a shortened grip on the reins, was little more than a recognizable blur as he came on. He had a sixgun on his hip and there was the butt of a saddlegun protruding below and behind the cantle on the near side.

Amos raised his carbine slowly, placed a thumbpad atop the gnarled hammer to pull back, and scarcely breathed as the man walked toward the front of the shed.

That curious milk-cow gave away, moving warily from the path of the oncoming man with the saddle-horse. Amos saw this from the corner of his eyes without heeding it.

He was poised to step out where the stranger could see him, when the stranger veered toward the shed. Behind him was a second man completely invisible to Amos until the horse turned sideways. In the dark this second man had been invisible. Amos hesitated.

The horseman walked up to a post near the door of the shed, tied his reins, then started to turn. Amos had a moonlighted look at the second man. He had a cocked Colt in his right hand. It was Bryce and he gestured for the stranger to walk over closer to the cow-shed.

Amos recovered from shock, stepped out with his carbine, and the captive saw him, saw that he was now between two men with ready guns—and slumped.

7

RECKLESS MEN

They took him inside, left his horse tied out of sight in front of the shed, and Bryce lifted away their prisoner's sidearm.

The man was burly, almost neckless with his bullet-head and thick, powerful shoulders seemingly joined together. He was unshaven and smelled strongly of horse-sweat. He offered no trouble, which was wise since he had a sixgun in his back and a carbine in front.

They herded him over to the south wall of the shed where side-boards had rotted off to allow more starlight to filter through, and there Amos poked his face closer, then pulled back as he said, " Jake Moran."

The burly man looked steadily at Amos from a lowered face, his unshaven coarse mouth pulled flat, his dark, small eyes venomous. He said nothing.

Bryce stepped around in front with his sixgun cocked and tipped. The burly man's small, malevolent eyes shifted from Amos. He seemed more interested in Bryce, but he still said nothing.

Amos eased off the dog of his Winchester and grounded the thing to lean on. " Where you going?" he asked the prisoner. " I thought that was your voice, a while back when the dog was barkin', and someone was talkin' to the sentry over yonder. You had enough, Jake, and figure to pull out?"

Moran remained fiercely silent, looking from one of them to the other. He reminded Bryce of a cornered bull the way he stood, thick shoulders sloping, corded, oaken arms hanging helplessly at his side, willing to fight but perfectly aware that he had no chance.

He said, "Yeah, I had enough," in a deep-down rumbling voice. "That damned fool's so busy playing king of the mountain, wantin' everyone to bow to him, he's ruined our chances. Manuel would have ripped this place apart by now, stacked you town-bastards like cord-wood in the road, and set fire to the place."

Amos smiled flintily. "Manuel's dead." He jerked his head sideways. "This is the feller who downed him."

The malevolent small black eyes blinked suddenly, in obvious surprise. "Him? He was here in town all the time, Amos?"

"Yeah."

Jake Moran looked steadily at Bob Bryce, then swore in a rumbling monotone, and said, "That dumb beaner. He never even caught on. You fellers was hoodwinkin' him about bringin' this feller back and he never caught on.' Moran let go with a hair-raising epithet and shoved both scarred big hands into trouser pockets, glaring at his captors.

Bryce eased the hammer down and stepped back as he holstered his sixgun. He met the savage look of his captive without blinking. "What does Halder figure to do?"

"Do?" exclaimed the angry, disgusted prisoner. "Play like he's an army general as long as he can. He's struttin' around in there givin' orders and drinkin' Manuel's whiskey. I told him we'd ought to raid the damned town before sun-up, not after. He said he wanted you —the feller who killed Manuel—and after the store-keepers fetched you in, then we'd burn the damned town and pull out."

"Did he know you were leaving?"

Moran looked disgustedly at Bryce. "Of course he didn't know. He'd have thrown down on me if he had known."

"The sentry knew."

"Sure. He wouldn't say anything. Hammer and me've been partners a long time. I tried to get him to leave with me. He wouldn't because we couldn't steal but one horse." Moran swore again. "I told the idiot Halder wouldn't come after us even if we left on foot."

Jake Moran stopped speaking, studied Bryce and Cody, then said, "What you fellers think you can do, hidin' back here in this shed?"

"Keep you from escaping," stated Bob Bryce, "for one thing. We've got other plans too."

Moran wagged his head. "If someone went for help it'll be a wasted ride. Amos here can tell you that. There ain't no towns with lawmen closer than a three-day's ride from Shepler's Spring."

Bryce moved away a yard farther and rolled a smoke, lit it inside his hat to hide the match-flare, then offered

Jake Moran his tobacco sack. The prisoner shook his head and watched Bryce with the gaze of a reptile. Bryce said, "How do we get in there, Jake?"

Moran answered tersely. "You don't. If you expect me to help you, forget it. I wouldn't give you the time of day."

There was no question about the prisoner's resolve. His entire appearance was of a man who could not be coerced. Bryce smiled at him, and that made the thick-bodied black-eyed man's glare narrow. "Pete'll kill you," Moran said. "He's bein' a damned fool right now, mister, but before this night is over he'll kill you." Moran turned, "and you, Amos. Unless you get on a horse and get fifty miles under you before sun-up. The whole lot of you are damned fools to still be here in town."

Amos turned enquiringly to Bob Bryce. They had a dangerous captive and nowhere to put him. Bryce kept half-smiling at the bullet-headed man. "Walk back to the door," he ordered, and when the burly prisoner stamped past, Bryce's gun-arm rose and fell in a blur. The sound was of steel over bone. Moran's old hat was punched down over his ears. He fell to the cow-shed floor without a murmur and Amos gawked.

Bryce leathered his Colt and knelt, pulling at Jake Moran's shellbelt. He also removed his trouser-belt, With one he bound the unconscious man's ankles and with the other belt he lashed Moran's thick arms behind the renegade's back. Then he rose and looked at Amos.

The saddlemaker was worried. "That was a hell of

a whack," he muttered.

Bryce did not even look down. "He's got a head of solid bone. Come along. I think I know how we can get inside."

Amos looked up with a swift scowl. "You're crazy. There are still four of them in there. You're not goin' up against a bunch of Sunday-school teachers. You heard Jake. They're loaded for bear."

Bryce stood a moment gazing at the saddlemaker without making a sound, then he turned, stepped over Moran and went as far as the door before turning to glance back. Amos met his look without yielding, and Bryce went out of the shed to the post where the patient horse was standing and started to untie the animal.

Amos went to the doorway to watch. Bryce did not glance back, but turned the horse and started leading it back the way it had come when Jake Moran had been leading it. Amos went back through the shed to watch from the cracked wooden wall as Bryce appeared over by the chicken house, then on around it back toward the ajar gate. He saw the sentry straighten up from a sleepy crouch and stare as Bryce crossed toward the gate. The sentry gradually turned to watch Bryce lead the horse back inside. Amos stared. What Bryce was doing was, in the saddlemaker's opinion, plain madness. But it also occurred to Amos that while the sentry had his back turned, was concentrating all his attention upon Bryce, it would be safe for Amos to leave the cow-shed. He turned, saw the inert man on the floor bound wrist and ankle, kicked the unconscious man's sixgun out into the yonder yard, then stepped over him and left the shed, swearing to himself about himself. What he was now doing went against every sane instinct he had.

Without effort he reached the alley, crossed it, went silently below the place where the sentry was, glanced up and saw that the sentry was still watching what he doubtless thought was Jake Moran returning, and hastened along the implanted poles to the gateway, both palms sweat-slippery around the Winchester he used to lever the gate farther open.

Bryce was looking back, straight at Amos, when the older man stepped inside the yard. The sentry leaned at sight of a second man. "Who's that?" he asked softly. "Jake, who you got with you?"

Bryce, holding the horse so that it partially hid his body, made a muffled effort to answer in a deep tone, and the sentry climbed down and started forward as he said, "What in hell did you come back for?"

Bryce was holding the horse close to the bridle with his left hand. When he turned the horse he had a sixgun showing plainly in his right hand. The sentry stopped dead still, his eyes coming up from the gun-barrel to the man holding it. Now, finally, he knew Bryce was not Jake Moran, but he did not make a sound as Amos stepped stiffly around to disarm him.

A man's sharp, hard voice came up to them from the middle of the corralyard. "Hammer, what's goin' on over there? Who's that with the horse?"

Bryce shoved the gun. "Tell him it's Jake and he's

fixing to leave."

The sentry's movement was jerky when he twisted to answer. " Jake's pullin' out."

The man in the middle of the yard ripped out a savage curse and started forward with thrusting strides as he called ahead.

Bryce gouged the astonished horse. It sprang ahead knocking down the bewildered hostler, then the horse turned toward the ajar gate and Amos gave a bound to avoid being struck at exactly the time the man coming toward them fired his sixgun. The bullet struck a log paling, beyond where the saddlemaker had been standing, with a solid sound.

Amos spun to follow Bryce as the up-ended hostler fumbled on the ground for his holster. Bryce was fast, and given this kind of motivation the older man was equally swift. They ducked over alongside the corral-yard bunkhouse as a pair of men rushed forth, guns in hand, but looking as though they had just awakened. They did not see the men who had just fled past, but saw instead two of their friends rushing forward with cocked Colts. Both the bewildered hostlers turned and hurled themselves back into the bunkhouse.

Hammer fired, presumably in the direction Bryce and Cody had fled, but the bullet was two feet wide and smashed the only window in the bunkhouse. Inside, someone cried out abruptly, then swore.

Bryce got back as far as he could on the west side of the bunkhouse, sank to one knee as Amos hurtled past into the upright logs beyond, and when someone

74

out front shouted for others to surround the bunkhouse, Bryce fired at the sound of that loud voice.

Amos waited for a target, saw none, and also fired out into the yard. They both levered up and fired again. The impression was of two very determined and well-armed men inside the corralyard. That man who had cried out from within the bunkhouse moments earlier, sang out again, this time articulately demanding to be told what was happening.

No one answered him. Hammer and the man who had come rushing from the middle of the yard were nowhere in sight now. Nor did either of them fire again.

Bryce stood up, looked around, saw Amos lowering his carbine also to stare, and went back another few feet where the palisaded corralyard wall became the rear wall of the bunkhouse. There was no way of escape around the bunkhouse. Bryce and Amos Cody were in a dead-end with their backs to the wall.

Amos went over alongside the windowless west wall of the bunkhouse, began edging toward a better sighting along the entire yard, and Bryce hung back just long enough to plug in two fresh loads to replace the ones he had fired, then he too slipped forward. There was no other way to go.

If their attack had not been such a total surprise, Halder and his remaining renegades could have pinned Bryce and Cody to either side of the bunkhouse, or that lofty log wall farther back. As it happened, Hammer had run for cover the moment Bryce fired, and the larger man who had come rushing forward, had sprang

75

onto the little porch of the bunkhouse where he had flattened against the rough wood, well camouflaged by darkness and shadows.

Amos continued to inch forward without any knowledge that someone was on the porch around in front. But Amos did not make a sound. He knew there were men inside the bunkhouse. He had some vague, desperate idea to get them out so that he and Bryce might get inside. The bunkhouse was the only shelter along the backwall. Out front was the entire open, exposed big corralyard. Normally, there might have been at least one stagecoach standing out there, greased and ready to go out. Now, there was nothing between the bunkhouse and the way-station office over along the front wall and north of the roadway gates.

Bryce, close behind Amos, heard sounds through the bunkhouse wall and reached to catch Cody's attention, then wag his head as a warning. Amos halted. Around front, that large man pressing flat against the bunkhouse front wall with its shattered window, had his sixgun cocked and raised shoulder-high, in the posture of a duellist. He was waiting. He knew Bryce and Cody were around there. He also knew they had no other way to escape unless they scaled the wall, and thus far he had heard nothing to suggest they were doing that.

8

DEADLY DANGER

The two corralyard invaders, with a moment of respite, had time to make an assessment, but they did it individually, with the obvious factor uppermost; they were inside the yard with Pete Halder and his companions aware of their presence.

They were also in a poor position. Their enemies knew where they were, and that to escape from around there they would have to expose themselves.

If there was an alternative to jumping forth, guns blazing, it probably was to scale the rear palisaded wall and drop back down into the alley, and that would be turning their backs on men who by now would probably have guessed that these were the only choices.

Amos, a yard in front of Bob Bryce, was in a crouch concentrating on what he could see of the empty corralyard, which was only the back wall, with a slice of the middle yard scantily visible.

The abrupt silence was lethal in its significance. Halder's renegades could be creeping up. Bryce leaned to whisper. " We better try the wall," and Amos acted as though he had not heard.

Out front, beyond the closed front gate in the roadway, or across it in the area of the saloon, someone called out in a high voice, his words indistinguishable. A moment later another man sang out, northward but he seemed to be on the same side of the road as the way-station.

A moment later someone fired a shotgun. It sounded like a small cannon, and that was the moment Amos chose to drop low, step ahead and thrust his head swiftly around the front wall. A gunblast nearly deafened Bob Bryce. Someone, probably that large, dark man who had disappeared from sight immediately after the first exchange of shots, had been waiting around there. But his slug missed Amos by a foot and ploughed up a great gout of dirt and dust fifteen feet beyond.

Amos swung his shoulders. Bryce could not see the gun but he knew Amos was going to fire. He did, and this time muzzleblast as well as gun-thunder shattered the eerie starlighted gloom.

Amos pulled back and twisted, his face pinched down hard, his eyes narrowed. He gestured toward the rear wall, but as Bryce started to turn back, that scattergun let go with its second barrel down in the area of the way-station office. This time, a rattle of Winchester fire came back.

If Mike, Simon and Henry Shepler were engaging someone who was inside the roadway office, it might become a diversion. At least this was Bryce's supposition as he turned and hastened toward the rear wall.

It was not much of a diversion but it was better than none at all. Bryce had to holster his sixgun and crouch

78

low to spring high enough to grasp the tops of the fence poles. He made it, his back a perfect target as he threw every muscle into his scramble upward. When he could straddle the topmost logs he did so, twisted back and palmed his sixgun as Amos came up, stepped slightly to one side, leathered his handgun and gave a desperate bound. He caught hold of the log-tops too.

Bryce, with no target, fired twice, once into the ground at the edge of the bunkhouse porch, the second shot out into the empty yard, his purpose being to discourage anyone around there who might have heard them, might have guessed what they were doing.

Evidently it worked because Amos teetered on the log-tops then dropped down into the alleyway. Bryce swung one leg over and fell beside the older man. They turned and raced for the nearest shelter, which was that hen-house where Bryce had been when he'd captured Jake Moran.

Breathless, dirty and rumpled, they got out there and flung inside. The walls were too flimsy to stop a bullet but they provided cover.

Amos had torn his shirt in the climb out of the corralyard. He had also lost his carbine but right now that did not enter his thoughts. He had to wipe clammy sweat from his palms, though, as he stepped forward seeking a crack in the warped old siding.

Bryce remained near the hen-house doorway watching. He had a perfect view of the ajar back corralyard gate. No one appeared over there, nor had he expected anyone to.

Around in the front roadway those carbines still sporadically fired but for a long while the shotgun did not reply. When it did, though, the noise was unmistakable.

Amos turned, finally, looked at Bryce and said, " You damned idiot."

The younger man gave no retort. He had gambled, and lost. That was the extent of it. They were both alive and uninjured, except for Amos's torn shirt, and the splinters each man had acquired in their wild scramble over the log wall.

Silence settled for a while, before a man called out in a distinct voice from the front roadway warning the embattled men in the corralyard that they could not get out unless they left their guns behind and walked out hands high.

This brought the shotgun up again. As its echoes diminished someone inside the corralyard also fired a Winchester. Clearly the call to surrender had not been received sympathetically.

Amos stepped back to reload his sixgun. He refused to look at Bob Bryce again until the younger man walked up and said, " I'll buy you a new shirt."

Amos looked at Bryce a long moment, then wanly wagged his head. " How do I get the ten years back I got scairt out of me over there?"

Bryce smiled. " You should have been a sheriff instead of a harness-maker. You put up a hell of a fight."

Amos kept regarding the younger man, the tightness

in his stomach gradually loosening. He wagged his head and ruefully said, " Like hell. Nobody shoots at harness-makers. . . . Well, if I had any grandchildren I'd have something to tell them wouldn't I?"

They decided to try and get back to the cow-shed, but not until that brush-fight out front brisked up again. Meanwhile they stood in the smelly chicken house recovering.

The sentry did not re-appear along the back wall across the alley. By now the renegades knew Bryce and Cody had escaped over the wall. It would take no great perspicacity to realize they were lurking out back somewhere and anyone who poked his head and shoulders over the wall might very well get his ears blown apart.

Bryce reloaded thoughtfully, emptying belt-loops one at a time. As he did this he said, " It's sure as hell a battle now, and they know it." He snapped closed the loading gate, turned the cylinder and leathered his Colt. " That's better'n waiting like we were doing before."

Amos probably did not agree because he leaned to peer out again, without uttering a word until he was satisfied no one was along the opposite log wall, then he jerked a thumb in the direction of the door. " Let's go," he said, and moved back.

The open area between the hen-house and the old shed where they had first kept their vigil, being devoid of any kind of cover, looked worse now to them both as they lowered in front of the chicken-house. Bryce said, " Maybe we'd ought to wait," but old Amos, still smouldering, would not have agreed with Bob Bryce if the younger man had said a profound truth. He shouldered past, gauged the distance, drew his Colt, held it dangling at his side, took down a couple of deep breaths and started running.

Bryce stepped around the side of the hen-house, raked the palisaded wall for movement or a human silhouette, prepared to give Amos support if it were needed, saw no one over there, and also lit out running.

Nothing happened. They made it to the cow-shed and sprang inside. Their belted captive had dragged himself over to a stanchion and was propped up over there in a sitting position. He watched them jump inside, guns in hand, and did not move a muscle.

They ignored him to step over to the front wall and peer out. In the front roadway someone let go with a handgun shot, then the scattergun cut loose again. Evidently Henry, Simon and Mike Reader were keeping the renegades occupied around there.

Amos leathered his Colt and turned a baleful gaze upon Jake Moran. The captive sneered. "Didn't make it did you? I figured they'd killed you both."

Amos's lethal stare went with his next words. "We should have hauled you along for a shield, Jake." He breathed heavily for a moment before also saying, "You're lucky. Those fellers in the yard don't stand a prayer of a chance."

Moran's sneer turned into a wolfish smile. "Wait and see, Amos. I never yet seen townsmen who were worth a damn in this kind of fight. Wait and see."

Bryce peered out, the palisaded wall was still empty of a sentry, there was no noise at all now, and as he turned he caught Amos's eye. "Let's take him out front."

Amos still was unwilling to concur with the man who had come within an ace of getting him killed. "What the hell for? That'll leave the back-alley wide open if Halder decides he's had enough."

Someone whistled from southward down the alley. Bryce moved away from the front wall as Amos went over there to peek out. Bryce hesitated by the doorway, then stepped out. Whoever was down there had palpably not come from the corralyard, which meant he had probably come from around front.

Bryce edged to the south corner of the shed. The cow whose shed this was, was standing back a discreet hundred or so yards chewing her cud and watching with a look of detached interest as Bryce leaned to look down the dark alleyway. He whistled.

Moments later whoever was down there returned the whistle. This time it was possible to fix the position of the whistler; he was on the west side of the alley not very far north of the shoeing shop, probably somewhere around that tumble-down old buggy house which was opposite the rear of the blacksmith shop.

Bryce waited, heard a faint sound and whirled to see Amos in the cow-shed doorway. They exchanged a look then Bryce whistled again. This time when the answering call came back the whistler had moved northward, up toward the cow-shed.

Bryce was reasonably certain it was one of the towns-men from the front roadway. Even so, he kept flat against the shed under its meagre overhang where the shadows were thickest, until he caught a faint movement out where he was watching, and palmed his sidearm as he watched intently.

Amos came down behind him, looked, grunted, and finally said, " That's Henry," and stepped forth to wig-wag with an upraised arm.

Shepler kept cover between himself and the opposite side of the alley as he crept forward, reached the cow-shed and said, " We thought they had you fellers."

Amos glowered at Bob Bryce but did not comment. " We got a prisoner," he told the blacksmith. " Jake Moran. He was fixin' to pull out."

" Dead?" asked Shepler, and Amos shook his head. " Trussed up inside. What was all the shootin' about around front?"

Henry looked around before answering. " Mike thought he was a strongheart and got too close to the front of the office. Someone in there was watching and cut loose with a shotgun. I never had any idea Mike could run that fast." Henry moved around to the door-way and peered in. Because his eyes were accustomed to darkness he could make out the sitting captive. Moran glared back and Henry said, " I figured he'd be the worst of the lot to deal with."

Bryce's answer was cryptic. " He might have been, if he'd stayed inside."

Jake snarled at them. " Wait. You fellers just wait."

84

Amos sighed and stepped inside. "That's what we been doing. So far your friends haven't done so well."

Jake Moran, stung by that, glowered at the saddle-maker. "It's not over by a damned sight. You fellers'll be crawlin' on your bellies before it is."

Henry followed the other two inside the shed, eyeing Moran with his customary expressionless look. "The first time I saw you, Jake, that Sunday morning you rode in, I wondered if there wasn't a price on you, somewhere."

Moran refused to answer. He turned so he would not have to look at them. Amos returned to the wall, looked out, still saw no one along the log wall, and heaved a big sigh. Henry looked through the cracks also, then said, "They're goin' to climb to the roof of Simon's building so they can see to shoot down inside the corral-yard." He considered the listening captive for a moment before speaking again. "Mike tried to talk them out. I didn't think it would work and it didn't. But maybe if we can pepper the yard and keep them down for a couple of hours they might soften up."

"Like hell," growled Moran. "They'll pick you off that roof like sagehens roosting in a low tree."

No one heeded the captive. Amos tucked the torn ends of his shirt inside his trousers. "I don't have many rounds left," he told Shepler, "and I lost my saddlegun over yonder when we were inside." He shot a reproachful look at Bob Bryce. "Otherwise, maybe we could get alongside that back wall and when they commence shootin' from across the road we could also shoot down inside."

Bryce pointed toward Moran. "Take his bullet-belt, Amos."

It was a sound suggestion and Amos turned to comply with it. Moran offered no argument as Amos re-tied the captive's ankles with his own nearly empty shell-belt, but when Amos stood up the renegade said, "You're goin' to get yourself killed, harness-maker. If you had a lick of sense you'd pile on a horse and get a long way off from here."

Amos looked down. "That's always been my trouble, Jake. Never had a lick of sense." He turned back where Bryce and Shepler were spying through the back wall. Henry Shepler straightened back.

"I think we can clean them out," he told the others. "That was a good idea, Amos—gettin' over where we can shoot down from out back while Mike and Simon are nailing them down from out front."

Moran snorted. "Yeah. If you don't get hit by a bouncin' bullet—or by Pete or the other fellers inside the yard. Go ahead and try it." He leered at them.

Bryce went outside again, remained out there for a short while and when he returned he was shaking his head. "There's not even a buggy out there we can push against the wall to stand on."

Shepler frowned in thought. None of them were tall enough to rise above the log wall without something to stand on. Amos too, whose idea this had been, looked disappointed.

Bryce then said, "But that back gate is still half

open."

Amos Cody raised sulphurous eyes to the younger man. That damned back gate had been what had enticed Bryce into nearly getting himself and Amos killed before.

Henry Shepler went out to look over there at the gate. During his absence Amos said, "If we use that gate, by gawd this time *I'll* do the leading!"

9

PERIL IN ALL DIRECTIONS!

The silence ran on. Bryce and Henry Shepler rolled and lit cigarettes. By tacit agreement they would do nothing until the men out front got atop the saloon, but it seemed to Bryce to be taking an inordinate length of time for them to get up there.

Henry shrugged that off as being inconsequential, until Amos returned from outside and said there was a streak of light along the eastern horizon. That inspired Henry to look at his watch. He spoke in surprise. " I thought maybe it was midnight or one o'clock. Hell, it's nearly five."

That milk-cow walked slowly toward her shed. It was getting close to milking time and she had a full bag. Somewhere southward a horse nickered in someone's town-corral. It was always a mystery that an animal which could not be taught to read a clock, could be so unerringly accurate about feeding time.

Jake Moran growled to have his hands untied so he could roll a smoke. Bryce instead rolled one for him, plugged it between Moran's lips and held the match. When their eyes met above the match-flare Moran's gaze was bitter. On a breath of exhaled smoke he said,

"What's the matter, mister, afraid to untie me?"

Bryce answered curtly. "No. But I don't want to have to kill you either."

Around near the back-alley gate they heard sounds and stepped outside to cautiously look over there. Nothing could be seen, and the longer they stood listening the more they were of the unanimous opinion that it was the stalled horses becoming restless and hungry.

Henry said, "Any darned fool had ought to remember to close that gate."

Bryce hoped aloud that no one would remember to do that, and moments later the gunfire came from out front. They stood listening to it but unable to see whether the gunmen were indeed atop Simon's saloon. Henry fidgeted. He felt his place was back in the roadway where he had been before. He mentioned returning to help Mike and Simon but old Amos spoke up, saying he would go instead. Henry shrugged, not happy but not prepared to argue about it either.

Amos hurried away southward and was lost to sight within moments as he strove to keep sheds and outbuildings between himself and the opposite side of the alley.

Henry dropped his smoke, shot Bryce a look, then leaned to make certain Jake Moran was still in there, helpless. As he straightened around to speak, the gunfire increased, some of it coming from inside the yard. Under these circumstances a man would have had to have shouted to be heard.

Bryce, watching the ajar gate, thought the renegades

would be fully occupied in front, and gestured for the blacksmith to follow him.

They had no difficulty reaching the log wall, nor in creeping close along it as far as the gateway where they halted to listen.

The embattled renegades for the first time this night, were not in a position to control things. Maybe, as Moran had said, Pete Halder had over-played his hand. When he should have ransacked Shepler's Spring and gone on, he had remained behind to swagger and emulate his dead chieftain.

Bryce got to the edge of the gate, dropped flat and peered around it from ground-level. He could see gun-flashes beyond the front log gate, could also see muzzle-blasts from scattered places inside the yard where men had evidently been pinned down unexpectedly by the overhead shooting which was lacing their area from above the front wall.

Bryce stood up and twisted to say, " We can get inside. But like Moran said, it's goin' to be risky; a lot of lead is coming straight up through the yard."

He led Henry Shepler inside in a sprint toward that side wall of the log bunkhouse, their nearest protection, in fact their *only* protection unless they chose to sprint southward among the horse stalls near the opposite side of the wall, a considerable distance, and over there while the protection was more extensive, it was no better. It might even be worse, with excited horses in those stalls.

Henry knew this corralyard very well. Better by far than his companion. As they settled against the bunkhouse Henry jerked a thumb. "There's a harness room and a granary on down this same side of the yard. Otherwise, there's no decent shelter, and the bunkhouse here is too far back."

But they remained against the log wall at their backs to catch their breath, and also to listen and assess the gunfire down near the front of the yard. It was as well they did because two men came darting and zig-zagging up from the front of the yard and ran inside the bunkhouse. Henry and Bob Bryce heard them in there, heard them rummaging and cursing evidently seeking boxes of bullets.

Bryce started to edge around Shepler so as to be in a position to flank those two men when they emerged, but Henry's thick arm came up to halt Bryce. Henry simply shook his head. Neither of them dared speak.

The men inside must have found what they came for because they suddenly ran out, darted down the opposite side of the bunkhouse and kept the other sheds along that same wall between them and the men atop Simon's saloon.

Henry said, "We'll get 'em. But not by standing twenty feet off and swapping lead and getting ourselves killed." He jerked his head, crept to the edge of the bunkhouse, peered around, waited, then led the way across the little porch and down the far side, the same route those two renegades had just taken.

Bryce saw the renegades before Henry did, pushed the blacksmith farther along where the darkness was lying in layers, then pointed.

91

The renegades were concentrating on loading a pair of rifles. Not saddlegun-carbines, but long-barrelled rifles which would have the range to reach the front of the saloon from far back in the corralyard where the shooters would be protected.

Henry knew the men. " Hammer and Gus Schilling," he said, and after considering the best way to get down there, decided they should wait until Hammer and Schilling were facing the roadway ready to fire and had their backs to Bryce and Shepler.

A bullet tore shingles off the roof of the bunkhouse. Bryce looked up, then scowled in the direction of the yonder saloon. Neither he nor Henry Shepler realized visibility was beginning to improve a little at a time as dawn approached.

Those two riflemen were finally ready. They skulked to the edge of the harness-room, looked out, seemed to be selecting targets, then carefully eased up their rifles to take hand-rests for accurate firing.

Bryce nodded. Henry started forward. If Hammer and Schilling would turn, they would have all the advantage because sixguns at that range were notoriously unreliable, and they both had rifles.

Henry and Bryce did not hesitate once they exposed themselves. Their only chance was to move swiftly. Even making noise was not important now, with gunfire sporadically erupting from inside the corralyard as well as outside it.

The renegades both fired. Across the road a piece of wood splintered and flew apart on Simon's false-front.

For a long moment no more gunfire came from up there. Evidently those rifles had scattered the attackers behind the false-front. Someone down near the office let go with a triumphant howl, and at once the gunfire from inside the yard increased. Halder and his men, grim and a little desperate before, now had reason to feel elated and to become more aggressive than ever.

Again those two riflemen aimed and fired, and again wood broke under impact across the top-front of the saloon. Someone called back encouragement to the riflemen.

Bryce drew his Colt. He and Henry were almost close enough to shoot handguns. Henry seemed to pause once, in mid-stride, waiting for the riflemen to stand up and aim again, then he abandoned a cautious approach and raced ahead, sixgun up and swinging to bear.

Something, perhaps instinct, made the nearest of those riflemen look over his shoulder before firing. He saw shadowy movement rushing straight at him and made a squawking outcry then tried to whirl, but with the heavy rifle to his shoulder there was not quite enough time.

Henry charged him head-on. His companion, a smaller man, quicker and farther off, looked, then dropped his rifle as he came around clawing for his holster.

Bryce swerved, fired from the hip at this one, missed by inches, but made the rifleman flinch, then try to whirl away. Bryce swung his Colt like a club. The man ducked quickly with his own handgun rising. Bryce lashed out with a wild kick. The man's gunhand was driven into the wood of the harness-room, the gun dropped and Bryce was on him swinging for his head. He grazed the man, knocked his hat off and felt the gunbarrel connect with a shoulder bone as Henry and the larger man careened sideways striking Bryce and nearly knocking him off-balance.

The smaller man—Hammer—swung a wild blow and hit Bryce in the ribs, but the strike had little force behind it. Bryce caught himself, balanced forward and drove straight into his adversary.

Hammer caught Bryce coming in with a stinging left hand, but when he moved to follow it up with his right, he flinched; it had been the right shoulder which had taken the force of that gunbarrel, and that hesitation allowed Bob Bryce to come in with a lashing right hand which half turned Hammer. The renegade was tough, or desperate; he came back off the harness-room wall with a well-aimed left hand. Bryce tried to get under it. Hammer's fist grazed over the top of Bryce's head knocking his hat away.

That was Hammer's last good punch. Bryce pawed him away with his left hand and fired his right. Hammer's knees went rubbery. He instinctively sought to turn away but the next blow caught him under the ear and he went back against the wall, and slid down it.

Henry Shepler was not as experienced as his larger, thicker adversary, but Henry was powerful; in solid condition. Shoeing horses, working a forge day in and day out, gave a man stamina and strength. Henry did not connect with his renegade as often as he had to absorb punches, but whenever he caught the renegade solidly, the man was rocked.

Bryce leaned to scoop up Hammer's sixgun to use as a club, but when he was straightening up the big man snarled and came at Henry swinging. Shepler took the first and second blows without stepping back. When the renegade came in for a better blow, Henry fired his right hand from shoulder height. The renegade back-pedalled, staggered, dropped both arms and seemed ready to fall. But he stood there, doggedly refusing to go down.

Henry walked in, hit the man again, and that time he went down. He rolled, too dazed to rise but not yet unconscious. Henry removed the man's sixgun, kicked the rifle out of reach and stood sucking air while he watched the renegade.

Bryce heard someone calling from down near the front wall. " Shoot! Damn it, Gus, *shoot*!"

Henry stepped over, retrieved one of the rifles, lifted it to his shoulder and fired off a round, high over the top of the saloon. Then he turned without smiling and said, " We got to drag these two somewhere."

They had the harness-room closer by far than the bunkhouse. Bryce hauled Hammer to his feet. He too was dazed but he could stand, which the other man could not do as Henry got him upright. They had to support both their captives as they struggled to reach the door of the harness-room.

A man cried out in alarm. Bryce glanced southward. A large, dark man was staring at him with a sixgun

95

dangling from his right fist at his side. Bryce did not wait, he let go of Hammer and yelled at Henry to hunt cover. Shepler let his renegade drop in a heap and sprang back around the harness-room.

One bullet struck the building. That was all. Bryce and Shepler waited for the fusillade but it did not come. Bryce made a good guess. " Empty gun." He crept back to the edge of the harness-room at the precise moment someone out front fired a rifle. Evidently Simon and Mike had also decided to abandon handguns and carbines and use rifles.

Henry looked into the cylinder of his Colt. It was nearly shot out. He waited for Bryce to look around into the yard. Then he cocked his Colt and moved up.

Silence settled for a moment. Bryce peeked out but the renegade was no longer in sight so he pulled back and said, " He's gone."

They considered. Their former adversaries were both lying around in front of the harness-room. Any attempt to step out and grab them again would invite gunfire. Nor did they have any idea where that dark renegade had gone.

Henry spoke in a calm voice. " Keep watch. I got to reload." He went about this methodically as though they were not in danger of being attacked from the rear or around in front.

Those rifles from across the road opened up again, each rifleman raking the yard twice before desisting, and this time as the silence settled Bryce raised a raw set of knuckles to push sweat off his forehead. For the first time, he noticed that daylight was not far off.

They had been fighting all night long. Bryce moved to make certain the renegade who had fired that solitary shot at them was not out front. The yard was empty, and with the improved visibility Bryce could clearly see the battered boards on the false-front of the yonder saloon. He turned to look elsewhere just as Henry finished plugging in his last load.

The unmistakable voice of Mike Reader called into the hush. " Pete! You've got half an hour until sunrise. We'll round up everyone in town and come after you!"

Henry spat, considered the yard, as much of it as he could see, then made a dry remark. " Everyone else in town? Hell; we're it!"

Amos bellowed too, from the front roadway. " You can't get out, Pete. If you quit now you'll still be alive!"

That call got a sudden rattle of handgun fire. Bryce placed it as being down near the granary; on the far side of the granary but above the office. Henry too had placed it, and because he knew the ground better, he said, " We got him, if he don't move and if we can get down there without Amos or Mike shootin' us. Come along."

There was a very narrow passageway behind the harness-room which Bryce would not have thought was back there because in most corralyards, including this one, the buildings were ordinarily built so that the back of the log corral-wall formed the rear wall of the buildings.

Henry had to twist his body from the waist to squeeze through, but Bryce, with narrower shoulders, only occasionally scraped wood as he followed the blacksmith.

Amos yelled at Pete Halder again. This time his tone was derisive. There was no gunshot in answer, as there had been before.

10

NEARING DAYLIGHT

The initiative passed to Henry Shepler who, in his taciturn, unsmiling way, acted more like a workman going about his job with confident capability, than a man who was risking his life. He emerged from behind the harness-room into a right-angled corner of solid wood where it was still dark, hesitated briefly then started forward again without looking around at Bob Bryce.

They held close to the weathered old log wall as they made for the granary. There was no movement on ahead, and no silhouette of a man down there. Bryce had misgivings. He thought their adversary was no longer down there, but Henry suddenly pointed with his left hand. It took a moment for Bryce to see what it was Henry had noticed, then a slight movement helped him discern someone edging along the angle of the building until he was in a position to peer around.

It was a mistake. The men atop the saloon now had good enough visibility to see into the yard. Someone across the road fired a rifle. The slug slashed, siding on the granary close enough to make the man down there jump and pull back. Henry raised his Colt and continued to move ahead. They were almost close enough for accurate handgun fire. Henry moved more swiftly, now, concentrating more on their adversary than upon not being detected. Finally, he did as he had done earlier; when he was close enough he started to rush ahead, to get well within sixgun range.

Their adversary was a large, thick, powerful-looking man. With his back to them as he started to steal over for another look into the yard, he made a perfect target.

Henry knew him before he stepped away from the camouflaging log wall, angling toward the man as he softly called into the lethal silence.

"Pete!"

The man did not turn immediately but he called back. "Bring that damned rifle over here, Gus. Where are those other two bastards?"

Then he turned.

Henry had halted less than a hundred feet back. Bob Bryce angled away a couple of yards. The big man had his Colt in his right hand at his side, but he had two men, wide apart, facing him with cocked Colts. Even if he could raise his gun, tip it enough to fire at one of them, there was almost no chance that he would be able to get the second one before he himself was shot.

Henry gave him a moment to decide, then said, "Drop it, Pete!"

The large man gripped his gun harder, for a moment, his face shiny with perspiration, and hat-brim-shadowed so it was impossible to tell what he intended to do. Bryce raised his gun-barrrel a fraction aiming for the man's wide chest.

The gun fell to the ground.

Henry did not gloat nor hesitate. He gestured back in the direction of the harness-room. " Walk. Slow now, Pete, and keep your hands in plain sight. *Walk* !"

The big man moved mechanically. As he passed Bob Bryce he looked intently at him from eyes the colour of midnight. Henry said, " Watch him," to Bryce. " I know for a fact he's got a bootknife."

But the large man made no move to risk his life. There was no doubt at all about the willingness of his captors to shoot, and he knew it.

At the harness-room with its little wooden porch and warped old wooden overhang, Hammer was struggling to retain balance by leaning upon the wall, but the other man, Gus Schilling, had not moved from the sprawl he had fallen into when Henry Shepler had dropped him.

Hammer turned stricken eyes and watched the approach of those three men, without seeming to care who they were. He was dazed and in pain, his legs were unsteady and he was unarmed.

Henry told the large man to halt on the porch, which the man did, and turned slowly like a wolf at bay facing his captors.

Henry said, " You wanted that feller who shot Manuel? Here he is, Pete. His name's Bryce." As those black eyes swivelled to the killer of Manuel Fuentes Henry also said, " Lie flat on your belly, Pete."

Henry stepped over, shoved his gun-barrel against

the prone man's temple and said, " Bryce, pull up his pants leg and get his knife."

Bryce kept an eye upon Hammer as he moved in to obey. He found the bootknife, a two-edged weapon with a black handle. He flung it out into the yard then felt inside the other boot-top. There was a belly-gun in a soft leather holster sewed inside that boot-top. Bryce palmed the little weapon. It was heavy, had one barrel above the other one, and looked to be at least a .41 calibre pistol. Bryce pocketed the thing and stepped back.

Henry also moved back. " Get up," he said to the large man. Then he looked around the empty yard, looked back and gave their prisoner another order. " There's one left. Cactus. Pete, call to him down in front and tell him to come back here."

The large man gazed steadily at Shepler. " He ain't goin' to give up."

Henry's answer was curt. " That's fine with me. We'll kill him. But first, we'll give him a chance. Call down to him!"

Big Pete Halder did as he had been told to do. His voice rang down across the empty yard very distinctly. The remaining corralyard-renegade had to have heard it because Amos from farther off, across the road somewhere, heard it and yelled back.

" You move out of that office, Cactus, and we'll riddle you!"

Henry swore at Amos's interference, but Amos could not know Halder had been obeying Shepler's order.

He looked at Bob Bryce. The younger man gestured for Pete Halder to get down on his belly again. When Halder hesitated Henry growled. Halder got down with some grunting as Bryce said, " You watch 'em. I'll look up their friend."

Henry looked a little sceptical. Amos, Mike and Simon were still on the roof waiting to catch sight of something moving. " Go behind the granary," he told Bryce, " and keep to the back wall. You'll have some open ground. Run across it and you'll be directly behind the office . . . Good luck."

Bryce moved swiftly. He was an agile, sinewy man. Getting past the granary posed no problem, but as Henry had said, there was open ground from the east side of the granary to the yonder back wall of the way-station office, and the light was getting brighter by the moment.

He waited, looking for someone atop the saloon across the roadway. If they saw him from up there he would probably look like one of the renegades. None of them knew him well enough to be able to recognize the difference.

He studied the office, the intervening distance, gauged his chances and decided they were a little better than fifty-fifty, for while the morning was arriving there was still no bright sunshine, and probably would not be for another hour. Also, he would run a zig-zag pattern. Finally, those riflemen atop the saloon had demonstrated no outstanding marksmanship earlier, so perhaps even with better visibility they might not be any better now.

He had to take the chance. First, he checked the loads in his sixgun, then he eyed the intervening ground for obstacles, and finally he broke away in a hard rush.

Nothing happened until he was less than a hundred feet from the office wall, then three rifles opened up almost in unison. He heard bullets striking earth on his right, and one slug struck the logs on his left with a meaty sound. The last one sent him sprawling in a tumbling fall that carried him ahead almost to the log wall which had been his goal. Momentum made him slide along the ground with a sensation of sharp pain somewhere below his hip-holster. It was bad enough to make him grind his teeth.

As he reached the wall the gunfire shortened. The men atop the saloon could no longer see him so they dumped lead into the broken windows and splintered roadside front door of the way-station, which was a form of deliverance, actually, because the solitary defender in there blazed back with his carbine, then later, with his sixgun, concerned only with frontal peril.

In that deafening noise Bob Bryce pulled himself up against the office wall, did not attempt to look around, and gradually ran a hand down his left leg to find the wound.

There was no blood but the pain was unmistakable. He did not even find any torn cloth, so he straightened against the building and leaned to feel lower.

His boot-heel was gone. Shot off as though it had been cut loose with a huge cleaver. That particular portion of his boot sole was devoid of leather lifts; even the cobbler's nails which held a heel in place, were gone.

His foot was more sore than his ankle, so evidently the wrenching off of the boot-heel by that bullet had violently twisted his ankle. He moved it and pain ensued instantly. But he was enormously relieved. His original thought was that he had been hit in the body.

It required a little time for him to decide how to favour that painful ankle and still get up to his feet to test it. It hurt, but oddly enough it hurt the least when it was in its normal forward position. He eased weight down upon it. When the leg was slightly to the left or right the pain became intense. When the foot was pointing ahead, there was still pain but much less of it.

He tested it several times, then turned to look along the wall. That savage exchange of shots had ended. There was almost no noise at all for the time being. Bryce limped to the south edge corner of the front building and pressed his head to listen.

Someone was inside the office restlessly moving. Perhaps he anticipated being stalked. That might have worked an hour or so earlier. It would not work now, daylight was improving by the minute.

There was no back-wall windows but there was a solid door from the way-station roadside office to the rear corralyard. Bryce got up next to it and leaned to continue listening. Now, though, there was no sound. Evidently that man in there they called Cactus was calming down after the latest exchange.

Bryce leaned past the door, barely. He could see across the road quite distinctly. If there were riflemen still atop the saloon they were being very prudent because he could not even make out a gun-barrel, and what he wanted was for them to open up on the office-front again to occupy the defender inside so Bryce could possibly open the door in the back wall without being immediately detected.

Although there was no way to see, nor signal to, the men across the road, there was one sure-fire way to anger them. He took slow aim over a hand-rest upon the edge of the back wall and fired into the small glass window above the door of Mike Reader's general store. Windows, glass of any kind, were exorbitantly expensive in places such as Shepler's Spring. They were symbols of status, and this one shattered into a hundred pieces when the bullet struck it.

Someone howled in rage and began firing into the bullet-pocked front of the corralyard office. Inside, that man called Cactus fired back. Whatever he may have wondered about the earlier glass-shattering gunshot, when two more guns joined the first one, he had no time to think of anything except avoiding being hit. Those rifle bullets could not quite penetrate the log walls, but they came through the shattered door and the pair of front-wall windows as though there were no obstacles at all.

Bryce listened for the defender to fire back. He eventually did, but not as profligately as he had earlier. Bryce listened, decided the man was selecting particular targets rather than firing indiscriminately, and thought he understood the reason for that—none of them had many bullets left. They had been expending them singly and in fusillades all night long.

Bryce leaned, gripped the door-latch, raised his cocked sixgun to shoulder-height, and during the slackening of the furious gunfire he shoved the door inward. It did not make a sound, at least not one anyone could hear, and it peeled all the way around.

Bryce hesitated until he heard the man inside fire his Colt out into the roadway, then he leaned from the waist, an inch at a time, cocked Colt still shoulder-high.

The renegade had created a barricade of cabinets, two desks, even some thick oaken cartage and bullion crates, over near the splintered roadside door. He was to the south of the barricade, closer to the log wall which provided a more reliable source of personal protection for him. He had his back to Bryce and the open rear door, was down on one knee with a sixgun pointed to fire, waiting for the slack-time he required to peek around the barricade before firing.

Bryce could have killed the man with one random shot. They were less than twenty-five feet apart, the office was a gloomy shambles with bad light, but the kneeling man had a broad set of shoulders.

Bryce waited too. When the angry riflemen across the road slackened their fire, perhaps to reload, the man kneeling near his barricade very slowly and gently began leaning forward from the waist.

Bryce watched. When the man was fully extended,

was in fact easing his handgun into position to fire, Bryce brought his gunhand around and down. He had the centre of the kneeling man's back dead ahead of his front sight. In a curt tone he said, " Let down the hammer, mister, and drop it!"

The corralyard renegade was stunned, was frozen in that awkward position, for five seconds. Bryce did not fill the doorway yet. He could kill that man over yonder as easily as batting his eyes. He did not want to kill him, but he had no intention of exposing himself just in case he had to shoot. No man in his right mind provides himself as a target when he does not have to.

Finally, the renegade began to lean back, to get his bodily balance again, and as he did so he eased off the dog, let it rest very gently against the firing housing. He did not drop the weapon. Like any good craftsman, he placed it upon the chair-seat with consideration. Then he turned his head.

Bryce hitched around, favouring his sore ankle, and said, " Get away from there, friend. Stand up and back along the wall. Keep your hands in front."

The man was craggy-faced, perhaps forty, dissolute-looking, stringy and pale-eyed. He did not say a word as he obeyed every order Bob Bryce gave him. But when Bryce yanked a chair out of that jumble over near the shattered door to lean on, the corralyard man slowly shook his head. Whether that meant he could not believe he had been captured, or something else, Bob Bryce did not especially care as he said, " What's your name?"

" Cactus. That's what they call me."

" Cactus, lean over there and yell out into the yard that you quit, that you plumb give up."

Cactus continued to stand there. " Anybody out there who'll shoot me?"

Bryce gestured. " I don't know. Go on over there and yell and we'll find out."

Cactus's greasy, lined and dirty countenance congealed into an expression of fear and reluctance. Bryce's gaze did not waver. For an additional moment Cactus stood eyeing his captor, eyeing the cocked Colt his captor let come down very gently until its solitary steel eye was pointing squarely at the middle of his chest, then Cactus shuffled over near the rear-wall door to yell out.

Bryce waited. He was satisfied no one was going to shoot. The men out front could not see anyone yelling out the rear-wall door, and back there, Henry Shepler, who would be able to see, had his hands full.

11

THE MORNING

They herded their captives out the back way, into the alleyway, and on their way southward they unbelted Jake Moran's ankles so he could join them, but left the arms belted behind Jake's back.

The air was cold, visibility was excellent, but there still was no sunlight as Henry and limping Bob Bryce drove their prisoners down through a refuse-littered vacant site between buildings, and gruffly ordered them to walk on out into the centre of the roadway. Cactus was reluctant. None of the prisoners were eager, but Cactus was the least eager of them. He hung back until Pete Halder had stepped into full view, followed by grim-visaged Jake Moran.

There was not a sound for a long while. Henry stepped to a wall-bench and sat down. He was bruised and tired. He was also glum and dour. When Bryce leaned against the building-front nearby favouring his sore ankle, Henry spoke without taking his eyes off the unarmed renegades out in the roadway. " I'm too old for this kind of damned foolishness."

Amos appeared across the road, first, his unkempt shock of grey hair as spiky and wild as it usually was.

Behind him came Simon, and the last man to show himself was Mike Reader. He was carrying a long-barrelled rifle.

Those three considered the bitter-faced renegades, said nothing as they approached them, then stopped to await the arrival of Shepler and Bryce.

It was an awkward moment for every man out there. Henry looked at Simon, who jerked his head in the direction of his shot-up saloon. Without speaking the prisoners were herded over there and pushed down into chairs while the townsmen waited for Simon to finish making his quick look at the wounded lawman in the storeroom. Then Simon leaned aside his rifle and poured drinks, shoved the glasses forward, poured one more, for himself, and as he raised it he said, " What'll we do with 'em?"

Mike Reader had his answer ready. " Hang 'em. Look at this town. Look at the front of your saloon. And they busted my glass window. They'd have killed every one of us!"

Henry eyed Bryce and asked about his injury. Because the younger man did not want to say he'd had a heel shot off, he passed off his limp by mentioning that he had sprained his ankle.

Amos Cody methodically shucked empty casings from his sixgun and shoved in fresh loads. Then he leathered the old weapon, turned, while raising his glass, eyed the dirty, rumpled, sunken-eyed corralyard-men, offered them a small salute and downed his drink. Amos was satisfied. Unlike the blacksmith, Amos had resisted growing old all his later years. This episode in his life left him feeling he was still a young man; at least as rough and capable as a younger man. Not one of those renegades was within ten years of being Amos's age.

Shepler's Spring had no jail, but it had what had once been a powder magazine. In fact Mike still kept a few crates of blasting powder over there, but the real demand had ended when the easiest gold strikes had been made years earlier. The powder-house was made of stone with walls three feet thick. It had no windows and a thick steel door. It had served as a jail in the past. Henry suggested taking their prisoners over there and locking them in. He also suggested going to the cafe for something to eat, and, he said, he was then going to bed and sleep for twenty-four hours.

They shoved and growled at their captives, herded them to the powder-house, and when they all squawked that they would suffocate, Bob Bryce looked around in there, detected dawn sky in a few places up through the roof-shakes, and shoved Pete Halder, the last outlaw to go inside, while Halder resisted the pushing.

They closed the door. Mike Reader owned the key and the lock. He made a great show of slamming the lock through the hasp, but there were tired men standing there upon whom something infinitely more impressive, such as the Second Coming, could have occurred without eliciting an arched eyebrow.

They went back toward the front roadway. A dozen people were milling over in front of the locked doors of the general store and Mike Reader, his mercantile instincts aroused, squared both shoulders and hustled over there to fling open the doors for trade.

Amos too abandoned the others. He lived in the back of his saddle and harness works.

Simon and Henry mutely took Bob Bryce along with them as they returned to the saloon where Henry, despite his earlier insistence that he wanted only something to eat then ten hours sleep, accompanied Bryce to the bar.

Simon mentioned the wounded man. He thought the man was very much improved. Henry was dour about that. " He couldn't have got much worse, so if he was goin' to stay alive he had to get better . . . Who shot him, Simon?"

Langley stared. " How the hell would I know?"

They had not asked their prisoners about this. Maybe it had not occurred to them, and right now Henry was not intrigued about it. He said, " Keep my glass full, Simon, I'm goin' to look in on your guest."

Simon snorted. He considered the wounded man as anything but his guest, and last evening he had made it clear he did not want the man back there in his storeroom. And a lot of good that had done.

Henry entered the storeroom, gravely considered the man on the rickety old army cot who was looking back, then Henry methodically rolled a smoke and lit it before approaching the up-ended grate at bedside. As he sank down he nodded, without smiling.

The handsome stranger acknowledged the nod with

just his eyes. His face was pale, but his eyes were entirely clear and rational-appearing. He said, "Is the war over?"

Henry exhaled. "Yeah. It's over, and we locked the corralyard-renegades in the powder-house. How you feeling?"

"Like someone that's been shot."

Henry nodded while considering the tip of his quirley. "Your name is . . . ?"

"Alan McDougal. Yours?"

"Henry Shepler," replied the blacksmith, raising his eyes to the younger man's face. "I own the smithy down the road." He went back to studying the tip of his smoke. "Mister McDougal, you're likely to be flat on your back for some days yet. We don't have a hotel nor roominghouse in Shepler's Spring, and you can't lie here in Simon's storeroom, so I expect what we've got to do first, is find you a decent room."

McDougal stonily studied Henry throughout everything Henry had to say, and when there was silence McDougal spoke. "The *first* thing we've got to do," he told Henry, "is to find the man who robbed me while I was shot and unconscious."

Henry raised guileless eyes. "Really? They took your money? Did you have a watch too?"

"Not a watch and not my money," replied the law officer. "My badge as a deputy U.S. federal marshal, and a warrant for arrest I was carrying with me. And after that, the second most important thing is—the man who shot me."

Henry smoked. "We got 'em all alive, so when we get around to it, we'll find out which one of 'em shot you." Henry studied the bronzed face of the other man for a moment. "A badge and a warrant?"

McDougal weakly placed his left hand over the upper shirt pocket on his left side. "Took the badge out of this pocket, Mister Shepler, and took the warrant out of my pants pocket."

Henry rose. "All right. I'll discuss this with the others. But right now, we been up all night gettin's shot at." Henry smiled from the doorway. "It takes a lot of sap out of a man just bein' up all night, let alone goin't through all the rest of it."

He returned to the bar-room. Bob Bryce eyed him. Simon was nowhere in sight as Henry returned to his place, hooked a foot over the brass rail and leaned. Simon had obeyed Henry's injunction, Henry's glass was full. As he reached to lift it he said, "Mister Bryce, you helped the town last night. We're right obliged."

He did not sound either profoundly moved by Bryce's heroism and sacrifice, nor willing to be any more congratulatory than he was now being in a cool, almost detached manner.

"We maybe could have done it without your help, but I sort of doubt it. Although damned near gettin' me killed inside the corralyard wasn't the smartest thing either one of us ever did, but we survived."

Henry turned and gazed steadily at the younger man. "I'd like you to answer a question for me, if you would?"

Bob Bryce smiled. " Fire away. I'll answer."

" Why did you come down across the mountains to Shepler's Spring?"

" To get my horse shod, and that's the gospel truth. I hadn't seen another town in a long while. Another few days and I'd have been put afoot, with a lame or tender-footed horse."

Henry nodded. " What I meant was—what brought you to the Piute Plains country. I guess I didn't phrase it right the first time. How come you to be in this part of Nevada at all? You're sure not a Nevadan."

Henry could see the stain of colour in under Bryce's cheeks. He understood exactly why the younger man was suddenly angry but in the face of that fierce, justified resentment about personal questions, Henry did not waver.

" Mister Bryce, I got reason for asking these questions," he said, and for the first time saw Bryce's gaze reflect sudden suspicion, sudden caution.

" What reasons, blacksmith?"

Henry considered. He had certainly roused the suspicion of his companion. Undoubtedly a more skilled interrogator would have been able to avoid that. In any case, it was done, and from this point on Henry was unlikely to get the particular answer he had been seeking.

It was not that Henry wanted to know *where* Bryce was wanted, nor how much bounty money probably was on his head. What Henry wanted to know was which crime had Bob Bryce committed, because in Henry's

116

view, there were some crimes which could not be forgiven, and before Henry committed himself he had to know what Bryce had done.

Henry remained expressionless as he leaned facing the sinewy, lanky man. "The town owes you, Mister Bryce."

"What's that got to do with askin' questions, blacksmith?"

Henry sighed in silence. "You object to answerin' them?"

"Sure. Anyone would object to havin' his private life pried into," stated Bryce.

Henry knew he had botched it. He only had one thing more he could do, so he did it. He fished forth the crumpled warrant and pitched it over in front of Bryce, then, as the younger man was diverted in surprise, Henry drew his Colt and waited.

Bob Bryce did not unfold the warrant for a long time, he simply stared at it. Then he turned in bafflement to say, "What in hell are *you* doin' with that thing? You're no . . ." He had seen the hip-high gun-barrel.

"What do they want you for?" Henry asked quietly.

Bryce kept staring at Henry Shepler. "Did you read the warrant?"

"No. Not yet. Didn't have no time to look at it last night. What do they want you for, Mister Bryce?"

"Where did you get hold of that thing, blacksmith?"

Henry studied Bryce, then cocked his sixgun. "One more time—*what do they want you for?*"

Bob Bryce picked up his beer glass, still refusing to

touch the federal warrant. "Horse-stealing," he said, tipped the glass in a slight, mock toast, and drank from it.

Henry said, "What else. They don't send deputy U.S. marshals after common horsethieves, Mister Bryce!"

Bryce flintily smiled at Henry. "Yes they do, blacksmith, if the horses a man steals happen to be fine, big valuable army horses in a cavalry corral upon a military reservation."

Henry said, "Read from the warrant—aloud." He still was sceptical, but after Bryce had read the charges they were exactly as he had said they were, and Henry motioned for him to push the warrant across the bartop.

He had to back-pace a couple of yards to be safe from attack while squinting at the warrant. Bryce did not appear to be the least interested in attacking Henry. He finished his beer, pushed the glass away, and yawned prodigiously.

Henry stuffed the warrant back into his pocket, leathered his pistol and said, "Care for another beer?"

Bryce shook his head. "I'm sleepy enough . . . Well . . . ?"

Henry leaned, felt stubble along his jaw and drawled an answer. "Your horse is shod. By now I'd say he's probably well rested in the bargain. If I was in your place, Mister Bryce, I'd saddle up and get away from here before the heat rises to make it an uncomfortable day for riding."

They stood side by side for a moment leaning on Simon Langley's bar saying nothing. Finally Bryce raised his head. " One question. Where did you get that warrant?"

Henry fished around, located the badge and dropped it atop the smooth old wood. " That feller someone in the corralyard shot thinkin' it was you—the feller lyin' in the storeroom yonder—I took this badge off him and that warrant." Henry looked around. " That's what I meant when I said if I was you I'd ride out and keep riding. If this one is close on your trail, there may be others."

Bryce continued to study Henry. " You didn't have in mind lettin' me get out there on the desert somewhere I never been before, and don't know anything about—then overhaulin' me with a posse?"

Henry looked pained. " Mister Bryce, right now you could be either Frank or Jesse James, and I wouldn't even walk to the edge of town to see you, let alone ride with a posse. I'm tired." Henry stared. " Are you goin' or are you going to stand around here?"

Bryce did not commit himself, yet. " You told Simon and Mike and Amos and . . . ?"

" I didn't tell a darned soul and the reason I took that badge and paper was so that no one else would know who that shot-feller was and why he's here . . . Last night, Mister Bryce, *we* needed your help. Today, Mister Bryce . . . you need *our* help. That's a fair trade I'd say."

Henry shoved out a large, work-calloused hand, did

not smile, waited until Bryce gripped his hand and shook it, then Henry disengaged his paw and nodded. " Southwest a couple of day's ride and you'll come to Las Vegas. There's even some trees and water and green grass in that part of Nevada. Good luck, Mister Bryce."

Bob hovered a moment longer. " What about the lawman, Mister Shepler?"

Henry shrugged. " Even if he could ride, which he won't be able to do for some days, if he went accordin' to what I can tell him—he'd ride north-east."

They exchanged a look, Bob Bryce nodded and pushed on out into the magnificent, sunbright desert morning.

12

DIFFERENT OPINIONS

Henry was sleeping like a log when someone banging on his front door roused him. It took a long while for Henry to sit up on the edge of the bed, rub his eyes, listen to that loud noise, and yell out.

"You want to knock in the door, damn it? Hold your horses, I'm coming."

But he dallied. As his mind cleared he had a hunch who might be out there and why they had come beating on his door. As he stood up from pulling on his boots he felt for his watch, looked at it, saw that he had been asleep three hours, and with a disgruntled growl stamped out, opened the door, pushed on out upon the porch scowling, and flinched at the dazzling sunlight as Mike Reader said, "By gawd, he's gone and rode off."

Henry went to a bench and sat down as he buttoned his shirt. "Who's gone and rode off?"

"Bryce!"

"Well, why shouldn't he? He didn't belong here, Mike."

"He's a horsethief!"

Henry finished with his shirt-front. "Who says so?"

"That feller in Simon's storeroom. He's a deputy U.S.

marshal an' he had a warrant for Bryce's arrest for stealing thirty army horses up in Colorado."

Henry raised his eyes. "A deputy marshal? You don't say. Did he show you his badge?"

"No. Simon came after me when the feller talked to him. I went back, and the deputy marshal said someone stole his badge and the warrant for Byrce while he was unconscious after he got shot."

Henry gazed down the empty, sunbright, pleasant roadway. By now the morning stage should have arrived. That interested him more, so he asked about it and Mike became very exasperated.

"Yas, the darned coach came in two hours ago. Amos was over there. He told 'em what had happened, and helped 'em unrig the horses. Henry, that's not important. We're bound to help this federal officer."

Henry nodded, spat into the geranium bed and cleared his throat. He had been sleeping like a dead man. "Mike, a feller rides in here with some big story about being in pusuit of a horsethief, bein' a federal officer and all . . . Me, I got to see the proof. Not that he mightn't be a federal deputy, but he could just as easily be the damned horsethief too, telling this story to get us all stirred up for some reason." He looked at the storekeeper, saw the flush of irritation, and said a little more, in a quieter tone of voice.

"And Mike, last night another feller none of us ever saw before came along and risked his neck to help us set the town to rights again. Horsethief? All right; if that's true . . . I'm no judge and you and I aren't no jury. We couldn't have done it last night without Bryce. Is that worth anything? Your store didn't get robbed and ransacked an' burnt to the ground did it?"

Reader stood a moment, then moved around to share the bench with Shepler. What Henry had said was certainly true. Most importantly, what he had said about the store not being ransacked and burned was certainly the truth.

"Well . . . what about this federal peace officer?"

Henry settled thick shoulders against the rough boards at his back. "What about him? You didn't see any badge."

Mike scowled at the ground. "He's not lying, Henry. I know when a man's lying to me."

"All right. Then he told you and Simon the truth. What the hell are we supposed to do about it? He can't ride, can he?"

"No. That's what he wants us to do. Make up a posse and go after Bryce."

Henry turned a sceptical gaze. "Leave town, all of us . . .? Fuentes likely had something like that in mind too. And Pete Halder. I'm not going to do it, for one. If there're outlaws around darned if I see any sense in us all heading out of town, leavin' the place empty and unattended except for some old men, some kids and women."

Mike Reader continued to stare at the ground. Clearly, he had come seeking Henry Shepler for support in his agitation over Bryce being a fugitive, and a sentiment Mike Reader had about law-abiding folks running down outlaws, and now he was having doubts put into his mind. One thing was fresh and vivid in his mind. The village had narrowly escaped devastation last night. Just the suggestion that such a thing might still occur, valid or not, was enough to make the storekeeper pause in his reflections.

He finally said, " Well; I don't favour thieves. Any kind of thieves. But I favour hold-up-men even less and killers least of all." He straightened on the bench. " Bryce has a long start anyway."

Henry nodded. He watched someone enter the distant cafe and was reminded of his hunger. But first he had to clean up, shave and change his clothes. It would not have been necessary if the cafe had been operated by a man, but it wasn't.

Far southward a freight rig was barely visible, perhaps sixteen, eighteen miles away across the glass-clear, flat emptiness of Piute Plains. A couple of times a month freighters brought in the village's supplies. Henry rose, nodded at Mike and returned indoors. He had no idea what Reader would do, and did not particularly care as he grabbed a towel, a chunk of tan lye-soap and headed for the wash-house out back.

An hour later, bathed, shaved, freshly dressed, Henry headed for the cafe. It was well past noon, the place would normally be empty, and that distant freighter did not seem to have moved at all. Their best speed, laden, was rarely as much as four miles an hour. This particular outfit might not even reach town before tomorrow morning. With any luck several kegs of blank horseshoes would be on it, which Henry had ordered from an outfit in Missouri four months earlier.

As he entered the cafe Amos turned, his spiky hair combed for a change, his shirt and trousers fresh, and his leathery cheeks recently shaved. They exchanged a look. Amos had a half eaten meal in front of him. As Henry walked over and sat on the counter Amos huskily whispered.

" Wait 'till you see her."

Henry looked around. " See who?" The place was empty. He knew Rosie O'Leary who had operated the cafe since the death of her husband some time back, and nothing Rosie could do to herself would make her appealing to Henry Shepler.

Amos did not respond, he continued to eat, shoulders hunched, long neck bowed, both hands busy.

The woman who came from the kitchen had grey at her temples, a strong, abundant physique, doe-soft very dark brown eyes, and a complexion which put Henry in mind of raw cream. He had never seen her before, and yet . . . Sure; yesterday he'd caught a glimpse of another woman when the trouble was starting.

She came over, met Henry's slightly widened look, and smiled. She was, she told him, Rosie O'Leary's sister. Her name was Elisabeth and she had come out to Nevada to visit Rosie. Amos was grinning foolishly without putting down either his fork or knife. Henry felt colour coming into his face for no reason, and that irritated him so he ordered without looking at the very handsome, mature woman. But when she walked back in the direction of the kitchen, he looked. So did Amos, and old Amos noisily sighed, then went back to eating. From the side of his mouth he said, " Did you ever see anythin' like that before in your life, Henry?"

Shepler grunted and turned his attention to the pie-counter across from where they were sitting. Rosie made the best pies Henry had eaten since his mother had died many years ago. And she always had a couple of them on the pie-counter. She was the only person Henry knew who could buy a bale of dried, shrivelled apples, do something to them, then include them into a pie and have it not only fit to eat, but thoroughly delicious.

Elisabeth returned with Shepler's meal. When their eyes met she said, " I've heard of the wild west, Mister Shepler, but yesterday . . ." She stood shaking her head at him. " I used to believe it was a lot of talk."

Henry did not have the heart to tell her that usually it was a lot of talk, and that since he could remember, and he had lived in Shepler's Spring all his life, there had never been a real, genuine gunfight.

Amos, though, could not allow a myth to die, particularly one which happened to be close to his heart, so he smiling said, " It ain't so long ago we had In'ians around, and plenty of highwaymen and all, ma'm. Things been tame now, though for quite a spell."

Henry looked at the harness-maker, turned away and started eating. Indians! Highwaymen! Darned old shockle-headed liar! When he happened to glance up the very handsome woman was looking straight at Henry with a wise, knowing little twinkle in her eye.

She walked back to the kitchen area and Amos craned to watch. Henry spoke in a low voice. "She's going to catch you lookin' at her like that one of these times and bust you right across the bridge of the nose."

Amos blushed and went back to his meal. After a while he said, "Mike and Simon talked to that shot feller. Did you know that?"

Henry knew it. If he hadn't known it he would have still been sleeping up at his little house. He grunted acknowledgement. He had not realized how very hungry he was until he had started to eat.

Amos said, "That must be the first deputy U.S. lawman we ever had in town, Henry. I don't recollect one before, do you?"

Henry spoke around his mouthfuls. "Where is his proof, Amos? Anyone can claim to be a lawman—or a preacher, or a undertaker, or even a harness-maker, if he wants to."

That shocked Amos Cody. His head came up. "You don't believe he's a federal lawman?"

"You saw his badge?"

"No. But then it was Simon and Mike he talked to, not me."

Henry said no more. He ate, drank two cups of coffee and had a piece of apple pie, then he rolled and lit a smoke, put down his money and rose. The handsome woman came out to look enquiringly at him. "Was the meal all right?" she asked.

Henry kept looking at her. There was not a single flaw that he could see. "It's always good, ma'm. Rosie's my favourite cook."

" Rosie isn't here, Mister Shepler. She went over to Carson City on a vacation for a few days. I'm the cook until she comes back."

Henry felt the blush coming again, so he hastily said, " It was just as good as Rosie's cooking, ma'm," and hastened out into the afternoon heat and sunshine. Behind him Amos snickered, rolled his eyes at the handsome woman and wagged his head.

" I'll tell you something, ma'm. As far as I know Henry Shepler's never even gone buggy-ridin' with a lady."

" He's never been married?"

" No ma'm. He inherited some buildings here in town when his paw passed on, including the smithy. He's run the shop since he came back from the army about twenty years ago."

Elisabeth smiled nicely at Amos. " More coffee, Mister Cody?"

Amos had already drunk four cups. Every time she called him Mister Cody he had another cup. He knew very well he would pay for it later that night; coffee worked on Amos Cody like beer did, but he accepted his fifth cup.

Henry by-passed the saloon to go down through to the back alley on the east side of town and hike out to old Hap Sunday's house. The old man was out front on a rickety old bench. He had somehow managed to carry his old black dog out there. The animal was lying out full length upon a ragged army blanket, absorbing sunlight. He opened one eye, studied Henry for a moment, then let the lid drop.

Hap smiled. Henry looked at the dog. " How's he comin' along?"

The old man's smile broadened. " He's eatin' good, Henry. Beat the floor a few times this morning with his tail. He's goin' to be all right."

Henry dropped to one knee, stroked the old dog, who again opened one eye briefly, then Henry looked up. " You all right, Hap?"

" Yes. Knowin' Colonel's goin' to be all right makes me feel better too. Henry . . .? There was a hell of a fight in town last night. Did you hear the shooting?"

Henry said, " That young feller who knocked Fuentes down for kickin' Colonel . . . They met in the roadway. The young feller killed Manuel. His crew figured to avenge him by ransackin' and burning the town, Hap. We fought them to a standstill last night. The young feller, Amos, Mike, Simon and me. We got 'em locked in the powder-house."

The old man listened, then squinted rheumy old eyes. " I been in a few of those shoot-outs, Henry. Of course that was an awful long time ago."

Henry arose. " You want me to carry Colonel inside for you? It'll be sundown soon now, Hap, and he's pretty heavy."

Sunday rose unsteadily. " I'd be right obliged to you, Henry."

The dog was indeed heavy. Henry carried him into the shack with old Hap shuffling along with the army blanket. They bedded Colonel close to the stove and as Henry went to the door the old man said, " I'm obliged. M'dawg's obliged too, Henry." He thought a moment, then added something. " Sure sorry to see that young feller leave. He was a decent, considerate feller and Henry, there aren't many like that left, are there?"

Shepler agreed with Hap and closed the door after himself.

On his way back to the centre of town he lit a smoke. Peculiar thing about human beings, he told himself. The damned things just weren't ever plumb predictable. Here was a young buck who stole the army's horses—to sell no doubt, there wouldn't be much sense to stealing them otherwise—then he refused to let someone kick an old dog and bully an old man, and got in a fight for his life about that.

" Henry!"

Simon was out front of the saloon beckoning as Shepler came through the roadway dust. At the porch where they met, Simon frowned. " That feller in the storeroom insists on getting up and heading out. He come here on the stage, so he don't have a horse. He wanted me to rent him one, but I don't own a horse and we got no liverybarn in town."

Henry stared, waiting for the rest of it. He did not own a horse either. If he had owned one he wouldn't have loaned or rented it anyway.

" I told him," exclaimed Simon, " the only using horses right here in town are across at the corralyard, and with Fuentes dead and Pete Halder in the powder-house, there wouldn't be anyone around who'd be authorized to let him take one from over there. You want to talk to him?"

Henry squinted past at the lowering sun. It was close to four o'clock. Bob Bryce had been gone since early morning. By now, on that big stout horse he rode, Bryce should be about fifteen, maybe twenty miles away. That should be enough distance. All the same . . . Henry shoved past into the empty saloon.

"Yeah, I'll talk to him."

Simon led the way, then hovered in the doorway of the storeroom as Henry explained their situation to the lawman. He concluded by shaking his head. " Mister, you'd never catch up in your shape. You got no business even trying."

McDougal acted perfectly rational, perfectly normal except when he would have swung his legs to the floor to sit up on the edge of the bunk, then Henry had to help him. Afterwards, with their faces close, Henry said it again. " You'd be doing good to climb onto a horse, mister. You wouldn't last five miles and night is coming on."

The lawman glared. " He's getting away. Where is that blasted storekeeper? He was supposed to organize a posse."

Henry sat down upon the up-ended crate which had been serving as a chair at bedside. " Mister, we went through a battle last night, and none of us are as young as we'd like to be. And most of us don't own horses . . . and you said you were a federal marshal . . . but

I didn't see any badge."

" I told you it was stolen from me!"

Henry nodded agreeably. " All right. If you say it was stolen, then I'm sure it was."

They looked steadily at one another. Over in the doorway troubled Simon Langley fidgeted. All he really wanted was to get that wounded stranger out of his storeroom.

Henry rose slowly. " No posse, mister, and no horse for you. I can't authorize anyone, a plumb stranger least of all, to go over to the corralyard and help himself to a stage-company horse. That'd be stealing, wouldn't it? There's no one else in town who can authorize you to take one of those horses, either. . . Mister, just settle back, get lots of rest, we'll fetch food to you, and when you're able to mount a stagecoach step, you can leave."

McDougal sat studying Henry Shepler. He did not say a word until Henry was over at the door. " You folks in Shepler's Spring are obstructing justice."

Henry turned. " No, we're not obstructin' it, mister. We're just too worn out after last night to do much to help it. . . Get some rest."

13

SOMETHING NEW

Henry ate an early supper. With him, feeding was cumulative; he could go for long periods without eating, without being conscious of hunger in fact, but when he finally sat down to eat he was ravenous. Elisabeth broiled him a steak nearly as large as a saddleblanket, then she made a salad, something he rarely ate because Rosie rarely prepared them. Vegetables were scarce in the Piute Plains country.

Elisabeth also brought him a bowl of pudding. She watched him eat until he raised his eyes, then she smiled and turned to depart. He brought her back around with a question.

"I didn't know Rosie had a sister. You been her sister very long?"

Elisabeth laughed. It came easily and fell like cool water over creek-pebbles on a hot day. "Long enough, Mister Shepler. I'm a widow. My husband died seven years ago."

He nodded. He knew about loneliness. "So you came out here. It must be a disappointment, ma'm. Shepler's Spring isn't much."

Her liquid soft eyes held his gaze. "I'll tell you a

peculiar thing, Mister Shepler—I love open country. I've always felt that way. My husband once told me I'd been born on the wrong side of the Missouri River."

" Desert country?" he asked, sceptically. " It gets hot here in mid-summer, and in wintertime there's snow and wind."

" And wood-fires," she said, smiling directly at him, " and good fragrances from the kitchen, and visiting around, and planning for spring?"

He forgot the half-eaten steak. " Yeah. Those things . . . I can't get it through my head that a woman like you could possibly like a place out in the middle of a desert plain. We don't even have policemen. We got a church but there hasn't been a preacher in town for twenty years."

" You have buggies or wagons?"

He nodded.

" And you have mountains north-easterward, Mister Shepler, and trees up there with springs?"

He nodded again, watching her eyes as she talked. She *was* a magnificent female-woman by gawd.

" Then couldn't you take a hamper of food and drive up there and spend a few days around the springs and under the trees, when you wanted to?"

" Yeah," he agreed, although he had never done it. " Yeah, I suppose so." He considered the steak, realized it was cooling and picked up his fork and knife. " Elisabeth. . . ?"

" Yes?"

" . . . Uh. Could I have some more coffee?"

He had not meant to say that, and in fact his cup was two-thirds full so he had to gulp it down before she returned with the pot. What he had meant to say was—would she, someday, like to buggy-ride up to the springs and trees?

When she leaned to fill the cup he caught a faint scent of lavender, which upset him. She straightened up looking directly at him. " You're not a heavy eater, are you, Mister Shepler?"

He gorged, usually, after being without food for any very considerable length of time, except this evening, so like a child, he nodded in agreement with her, when he shouldn't have agreed at all.

" I was wondering, Elisabeth—how long is Rosie going to be over in Carson City?"

" A few days. At the most a week. You miss her cooking?"

He looked up swiftly. " Lord no. Well, Rosie's a fine cook, but so are you. Anyway, what I was going to ask is—how long are you going to be in town?"

She looked briefly out the front window into the dusky, quiet and empty roadway, her gaze pensively shadowed and soft. " I don't know. I wanted to see Rosie. My plan was to visit California." She brought her eyes back to his face. " Mister Shepler, I gave away my son last month in Cincinatti. He was twenty-three and married a beautiful girl back there. . . Three years ago my other child, Lili, got married too. . . . A mother's love is very powerful, Mister Shepler, but sometimes a mother needs to be a woman, to live out a few things she's always wanted to do." The slow smile came, soft and wonderful. Henry's steak was cold and his coffee was cooling too.

" I'm living out my lifelong desire to find wide, empty country with quiet and peace and beauty."

He cleared his throat thinking of last night. " Well, usually it's like that around here, Elisabeth."

She kept looking at him. " I don't know how long I'll stay. Certainly until my sister returns." She looked at his ruined meal but did not admonish him as she picked up the plate. " I'll re-heat this, Mister Shepler."

He arose. " All right, ma'am. But right now I'm not very hungry." At her mildly disappointed look he hastily said, " But if you'll get it hot again in the morning I'd sure admire to eat it for breakfast."

She laughed at him.

Outside, Henry, who was not a freely blasphemous man, sucked back a big breath of evening air, let it slowly out and said, " Gawddamn," then turned in the direction of the saloon.

Simon and Amos were discussing the cost of feeding the prisoners when Henry walked in. Simon set up a mug of beer, then said, " What're we goin' to do with them? The nearest judge is a hundred miles from here."

Amos, who had been advocating taking one of the stage company's coaches and transporting the prisoners where there was at least an authentic jailhouse, offered to drive the rig providing someone would go along as gunguard, and Amos kept looking directly at Henry.

The blacksmith wasn't thinking of his friends, nor of

their prisoners. He sipped beer, considered his craggy, strong face in the backbar mirror, turned finally with a grunt and watched as Mike Reader crossed toward them from the roadway door.

Reader's appearance had saved Henry from having to make a decision, and now, as the others told Mike their views and feelings, Henry was again left out, which did not disappoint him in the least.

He finished the beer, shoved the glass away, listened to the heated discussion of his friends, and went around behind the bar and out into the storeroom where the wounded lawman was sitting up drinking a glass of water as Shepler walked in.

They exchanged a look, the lawman set aside his emptied glass, remained propped on one arm and said, " I'd like to get a message telegraphed to Denver, Mister Shepler."

Henry nodded. " It can be done. We'll hand it to the next stage-driver going north, and he can send the message for you from any of the towns up north that have telegraph offices. All you have to do is write it out, Mister McDougal."

The handsome lawman relaxed a little. Lately, his attitude towards the townsmen had been one of noticeable but restrained hostility. " I'll write it," he told Henry, then also said, " I've got to get someone down here to help me find Bryce."

Henry sat down upon the up-ended crate without speaking. A full day had passed. A full night was ahead, and tomorrow there would still be no pursuit. Hell, if

Bob Bryce had simply *walked* his horse, by now he had ought to be far enough away.

McDougal's steady gaze lingered on Henry Shepler. "I can't understand why someone in Shepler's Spring would steal the warrant. Maybe they'd take the badge out of curiosity: as a sort of souvenir. But not the warrant. It's just a piece of paper. Mister Shepler . . . ?"

Henry shrugged. He had a distinct feeling that he was being baited. "It may be as you say—a souvenir."

"Who would do it?" McDougal enquired, still watching Henry closely.

The feeling was stronger now. Henry considered the younger, taller man with an almost clinical interest. "You must have some idea, Mister McDougal. You're a lawman, you'd come closer to making a good guess than any of us. What do you think?"

McDougal's gaze showed hard irony. "I think the man who took those things, Mister Shepler, probably didn't do it because he cares a damn about souvenirs. He cared about seeing to it that Bryce got away, with a hell of a big head-start."

They sat looking steadily back and forth. Henry finally shrugged. "None of us ever saw Bob Bryce before in our lives until he rode in here to get his horse shod."

"But after that, Mister Shepler, Bryce helped you gents save your town. That'd be a hell of an incentive to help an outlaw, wouldn't you say?"

Henry fished for his makings, tipped his head down and thought. By the time he was ready to light up,

138

Marshal McDougal had something more to say.

"An outlaw doesn't change overnight, Mister Shepler. I don't care how much folks are beholden, letting one get away only encourages an outlaw to break the law somewhere else."

Henry knew all these arguments and he still had no regrets. He trickled smoke and said, "Marshal, have you ever been married?"

McDougal blinked. "Married? No. What's that got to do with what we're talkin' about?"

"Nothing, I guess. It was just in my mind." Henry smiled at the federal officer. "You travel around a lot, Marshal, meet folks and see things, get some ideas about life and all . . . Tell me something: Is forty-five too old for a man to get married?"

Alan McDougal leaned there staring. He looked at the door, at the storeroom shelves, then back. "You. . . ?"

"Yeah. It's kind of silly I guess, isn't it?"

"No, I don't think so . . . But I'm sure as hell no authority. But it seems to me age don't have much to do with it, when a man wants to get married. Unless of course he's *real* old . . . Mister Shepler—about what we were talking about first . . ."

Henry rose, knocked ash, put a special look upon McDougal and said, "He's plumb gone, Marshal. He helped us save this town. It's not much of a place, but it sure beats campin' in the ashes those sons of bitches from the corralyard would have left . . . He's got about ten hours start. By tomorrow it'll be that much more.

Marshal, I sure wouldn't stop you from going after him if that's what you've got to do—but I sure wouldn't lift a finger to help you either."

McDougal was not angered. By this time he had certainly figured out that there had been more behind the town's refusal to form a pursuing posse, than just a lack of horses and saddles.

" I guess in your boots I'd feel the same way," he told Henry. " Anyway, it's got to be done. I'll write that message and if one of you gents'll come back directly, I'll have it ready."

McDougal eased his legs to the floor, straightened up very gingerly, and as Henry watched with interest from the doorway, the lawman lowered his head a little. He'd had a sudden surge of dizziness.

Henry closed the door very gently, stood beyond it a moment putting some random thoughts together, then went back out front where he winked for Simon to set up another beer, then he dropped the smoke and rubbed it out.

Mike Reader was no longer there at the bar but Amos was, and his usual candid, open expression was clouded by something resembling disgust. He said, " Henry, that damned storekeeper don't want to ante up for part of the hire of the stagecoach to haul the prisoners away, and by gawd that just isn't right. He's got the best building in town, and it wasn't burnt down. Just some busted glass is all."

Simon looked at Henry with a resigned shrug, and reached for the whiskey bottle in front of Amos to set it barely within the harness-maker's reach. Amos had already had enough.

The barman said, " How's McDougal?"

" Cantankerous," stated Henry leaning on the bar. " Righteous as all hell—but maybe he's entitled to be like that. Anyway, unless he can sprout wings he's not going to overtake Bryce." Henry hoisted his glass half way and smiled without a lot of humour. " Here's to Bryce."

Amos and Simon both drank. But in Amos's experience one toast called for a second toast. " Here's to Shepler's Spring," he intoned, holding a shot glass which was nearly hidden inside his big fist. " She's still standin' by gawd."

They drank to that also. Amos stared at Simon as though it were now his turn. Simon floundered, then came up with something. " Here's to the gov'ment lawman, may he recover right quick and get the hell out of my storeroom."

Henry finished his beer on that toast, turned to depart, and glanced back once at Amos, who was leaning upon the bar as though he actually did need its support. He winked at Simon and stepped forth into the beautiful early summertime night.

There was abundant damage in sight, by daylight at any rate, although most of it was not completely discernible by starlight. Otherwise the village was quiet with a faint, aromatic scent of cooking-fires in the night air. To Henry, who had spent most of his life here, things were taken for granted, and none of them, including the old weathered buildings, looked the least bit picturesque or romantic to him.

He liked the place, perhaps primarily because he had never got to know any other village or town, but he was perfectly aware of its shortcomings so he had no illusions. Nor was he by nature the kind of man who would rush forth to make excuses for Shepler's Spring. No one had to remain here if they preferred not to. To Henry it was satisfactory, warts and all. He shuffled up in the direction of the little clapboard house his parents had bequeathed him.

Someone was strolling north of town like a pale wraith, moving slowly with a measured stride upon the yonder desert plain. Henry halted at his front gate to watch. The stroller halted, looked at the great spread of vaulted heaven, stood like that a moment or two, then turned to walk back, slowly.

Henry had done that, in years past, walk out away from town and smell wild flowers, listen for the distant sounds, sense the presence of nocturnal varmints, owls and rats and little rusty-red foxes.

He knew who was out there and walked to meet her up where the plank-walk ended and the desert began.

She heard him coming and halted motionless. Then, recognizing his outline she allowed him to get within fifty feet as she said, "There is nothing here, Mister Shepler. You can turn your back to the town, look northward, or to the west and east, and see nothing which did not look exactly the same hundreds and thousands of years ago."

She was softly smiling as he walked closer. "There are some things which have always been here, ma'm, and which still are—like prairie-dog holes that folks walking out here in the night lookin' up can bust an ankle in. And snakes. Not at night, but they're here too."

Her smile faded a little. "You don't like it here, do you?"

It was his turn to smile. "Yes'm, I'm very fond of the desert. I'm even fond of Shepler's Spring. But it seems strange to me that a woman . . . like you . . . could possibly like the town or the Nevada desert."

"And you say all those derogatory things to discourage me?"

That was true, of course. That was exactly why he said them. Well, not *exactly* because he wanted to discourage her, but to leaven her sudden love affair with the Nevada desert because it would not always be late springtime, a period when all deserts are at their most appealing.

"I'd like you to see the country at its worst too, ma'm, and at its hottest, its wettest, and its windiest."

She kept gazing at him. "Do you want me to *like* it; is that it?"

"I'd just like you to see it all through its annual seasons. That's all."

She moved a few steps closer. "Does the desert make people practical, Mister Shepler?"

He grinned when she did. "I guess that comes from starin' at the bottom of so many horses' feet, Elisabeth."

She pointed toward the west. " All desert?"

" It depends on how far you go. No, there is a green belt over there a few hundred miles." He turned and jutted his chin northward. " It's green up there, in places." He paused, then spoke again, this time without facing her. " I'd like to show you a place up there called Shingle Springs. And another place where In'ians used to live centuries ago. They made a rock village under some cliffs up there, sort of like a hotel. There's a little creek and a lot of grass up there."

She said, " I'd love to see those places, Mister Shepler. When?"

That made him falter. He'd meant ' someday '. Clearly, she was not a procrastinator. As they turned back toward town he said, " Well, right after your sister gets back."

He walked her back to the cafe without seeing Amos Cody and Simon outside the saloon. Amos was sagging and Simon was trying to prop him up, pointing the harness-maker in the direction of his shop. He gave Amos a very gentle nudge to get him untracked, and Amos began moving. His progress was precarious all the way but he got to the doorway of his shop.

Simon turned, then, and watched Henry and the handsome woman down in front of the cafe. Simon stood a while before going back inside to lock up for the night. Nothing happened, he told himself, ever, in Shepler's Spring. Then hell, it all happened at once!

Henry might have had that thought too, if he'd been inclined toward philosophical generalizations tonight.

Instead, he crossed to the blacksmith shop to make certain the place was locked, then he went ambling northward toward his cottage, hands thrust deep into trouser pockets thinking of something he had never seriously considered before in his life. Being a married man.

This time when he went to bed he bolted the front door, not that he expected Mike Reader to come banging on it again, but just in case *someone* did.

14

MEN—AND A WOMAN

In the morning the town looked passable until the sun rose and all the broken windows, splintered wood and bullet holes were visible.

To Henry, whose ability to observe had got side-tracked even before he headed for the cafe, Shepler's Spring looked as it had always looked, except perhaps that the roadway window at Rosie's cafe sparkled from a vigorous, very recent scrubbing, and when he went in to claim that re-heated steak he found Amos there again, but not as vigorous as he had been the day before. In fact when he turned to see who had entered, Amos moved as though he were balancing a fishbowl under his hat.

Henry dropped down upon the bench, winked at Amos, who did not wink back but hunched to return to his breakfast, and when Elisabeth came for Henry's order her hair shone, her face was softly, gently smiling, and Henry was once again troubled by the most bizarre, indefinable and difficult emotion he had ever experienced.

He said, "The steak, ma'm," and she cocked her head, then returned to the kitchen without a word.

While she was gone Simon walked in, fresh and clean and solemn as a judge. He cast a look of sidelong reproach at Amos, who ignored Simon altogether, then as the barman sank down beside Henry he said, "The morning coach just arrived. I had to explain why there were no hostlers and that they'd have to do their own changing and all." Simon sighed. "What'll the company do? It don't even have a corralyard boss left in Shepler's Spring."

Henry thought of something else; that note McDougal was to write and have the stagers take up-country for transmittal. "How long'll they be?" he asked the barman.

Simon's answer was short. "Unless they stop cussin' and complaining and start changing hitches, they'll be two hours."

Henry turned as Elisabeth returned with a stack of golden brown pancakes, butter, and a pitcher of maple syrup. She placed the dishes before him, raised her head slowly, their eyes met, and Simon, seated close by watched, his eyes widened in surprise, and when Elisabeth turned to take Simon's order the barman bobbed his head. "The same thing, ma'm." Then he did as Amos had done, he leaned to watch her walk back to the cooking area.

Henry slathered butter and syrup, cut down through the stack of cakes, felt Simon's stare and swung his head. Simon said, "Amos told me about her, but he didn't say she could make pancakes like that."

Henry went back to his meal. Upon his far side Amos

finished, needed one more cup of black coffee to fire his deep-down burner, and when Elisabeth brought it Amos looked up at her with the hang-dog expression of a hound. "Thanks, ma'm. I really need that stuff today."

Mike Reader walked in, apron rolled and tucked inside his waistband. The others looked up but no one had anything to say until Mike leaned and gestured.

"That deputy U.S. marshal's leanin' in the doorway of the saloon looking like he's dead and afraid to lie down."

Henry felt Simon come up to his feet on the right, and as Simon turned hurriedly toward the door, Henry kept looking at his stack of pancakes. Then he muttered something vile under his breath and also rose heading for the doorway.

McDougal's face wasn't pale, it was very red and he was perspiring hard. By the time Simon and Henry Shepler reached him McDougal was prepared to try again to pass through the doorway.

Henry, strong as oak, blocked his passage. "There won't be a wall to lean on," he said. "You couldn't make it across the road, Marshal."

They turned him, got their arms into position of support and practically carried him back to the storeroom. As they eased him down McDougal raised troubled eyes. Henry, not very sympathetic, said, "What the hell were you trying to do?"

"Get on the stage—and head north for some help," the peace officer replied.

They got him back out full length atop the cot. Simon removed his hat and wagged his head. "You want to bust open your side and maybe bleed to death, damn it all?"

Henry pulled over the up-ended crate to sit on. "Write the note and I'll have the whip take it north with him. Marshal, that's the best you're goin' to be able to do for a few days."

McDougal slowly reached for a shirt pocket, brought forth a folded slip of paper and handed it to the blacksmith. Then he closed his eyes.

Simon led the way out front to his empty bar-room. "That idiot," he exclaimed. Henry nodded and did not even stop until he was across the room going out the door. "This town is getting bad, Simon. A man can't even finish breakfast."

He walked briskly southward, and when he got down there Amos was gone but there were two stagers eating like horses. They did not even look up when Henry dropped down at his place again. This time he went to work on the pancakes with the grim resolve of an individual who could not be torn away again by a team of horses.

The freight outfit arrived upon the outskirts of town, announcing its arrival by the braying of mules. Henry went right on eating. Those stagers sidled over for more details of the corralyard battle, and Henry said from the side of his mouth for them to go up to the saloon and ask Simon.

Nothing interfered with his meal this time. When he

was finished, and Elisabeth had brought him a second cup of coffee, he settled back to make a smoke to go with the java, and to wait out the other diners, intending to sit there until noon if necessary, until they had departed. It did not take that long. When the last diner departed Elisabeth came to lean in the kitchen doorway, rosy-cheeked from the heat back there, and ask if he had enjoyed the hotcakes. He was about to answer when Simon poked his head in to ignore Henry and say: " Ma'm, we need another bunch of stew-bowls of grub for the prisoners," then, spying Henry sitting there, he also said, " And when you got them ready, you can give them to Henry so's he can take 'em to the powder-house . . . Thank you, ma'm."

After Simon pulled back to go hastily back to his bar, Elisabeth saw the look on Henry's face, and laughed. Henry considered a moment, then smiled up at her.

She started to turn back into the kitchen as Henry arose. He said, " The moon had ought to be a little bigger tonight, if folks went strollin' out over the desert."

She looked back. " What time?"

He was becoming accustomed to her forthrightness, her lack of procrastination, so he said, " About the same time as last night. I'll be watching for you to close the cafe for the night."

She went on into the kitchen and Henry went outside to gaze down where the freighter was parked, tongue on the ground, hobbled big handsome, and very valuable, Missouri mules hunting wisps of bunchgrass, the man himself and his beanpole-swamper, gathering faggots.

There was still plenty of daylight in this particular day; the freighter could easily have hauled on in, unloaded at the plank-walk out front of Reader's store, then pulled beyond town to make camp.

Freighters were men whose entire existence was set to the snail-pace of long hitches of horses, mules, and sometimes oxen, although there were extremely few cattle teams any more. If the men had ever been impatient, after enough years of sitting high atop a wagon staring at horizons which never came any closer, inevitably the men lost something, became as phlegmatic as their animals. One day more or less, or even ten days, did not make one bit of difference. These men for example, could camp within shouting distance of the stores where they would deliver cargo tomorrow, and not be the least bit concerned that Henry Shepler might be in dire need of these four kegs of blank shoes.

Over at the corralyard there was a light in the shot-up, splintered office, and the roadside gates which had been closed, were now wide open. Henry could imagine the language those stagers were using over there as they surveyed the wreckage.

He saw a tall man leaning upon the rack out front of Simon's place and strolled up there. He thought he recognized the silhouette, and was wrong; it wasn't Amos, it was Marshal McDougal.

Henry sighed and wagged his head. They gazed at each other briefly before the deputy federal marshal said, " I'm being careful, blacksmith."

There was no point in arguing. If McDougal thought

he was up to it again, the same day, arguing was not going to dissuade him. Still, Henry had to make one caustic remark.

"You start bleeding, Mister McDougal, and this time you'll likely bleed out."

The tall man thinly smiled. "I did some re-bandaging this afternoon. I think it'll hold." Then, before Henry could dwell further upon this topic, the lawman also said, "I'm waiting for Mister Langley. We're going over to look at the prisoners in the powder-house."

If McDougal could walk that far without caving in, he was probably ready to ride a stage, if not a horse. As far as Henry was concerned, Marshal McDougal could do as he liked. He asked if McDougal would care for a drink. The marshal smiled. "No thanks . . . I already had a couple." There was a barely discernible twinkle in his eye as he saw Henry's expression of faint disapproval.

Henry entered the cafe leaving McDougal out there, and nearly collided with Simon who was on his way down to the cafe for those bowls of stew for the prisoners. Simon said, "Did you see the deputy marshal out front?" and when Henry nodded, the barman made a slight grimace. "He's pig-headed, Henry."

That did not have to be said. Henry headed past for the bar where a gangling young man Simon employed occasionally as a bar-keeper, was doling out drinks to a pair of unwashed, unshorn freights plus three pedlars who had arrived on the late-day stage. These five patrons of the bar were completely absorbed by the story of daring and risk and heroism Amos Cody was telling, complete with flashing eyes and great flourishes.

Henry watched for a moment, then nodded when the barman brought his usual glass of beer. The last time he had seen the harness-maker, Cody had been suffering. For a man his age he had to have great resilience. Or maybe those enthralled listeners down there were keeping Amos primed during his harrowing recitation.

Reader arrived, having closed the store, and for once Mike was perfectly willing simply to lean there, nurse a drink, and act composed. When Henry mentioned the lawman being up and around again, Mike said, "Simon'll be happy to get him out of the storeroom," and downed his glass of beer, thumped the bartop for a re-fill, and let go a big, wet sigh. "Reaction hits folks differently, Henry. A day later, and I'm just now beginning to realize how close we all came to getting killed. It's enough to make a man wilt."

Henry sipped beer, thought he liked Mike wilted better than Mike Reader acting normal, and rolled a smoke. There was an old clock above the back-bar. From time to time Henry glanced at it.

He was having his second glass of beer when McDougal and Simon returned. The lawman had no spring in his step but otherwise he seemed strong enough. He and Simon went to a table, sat down and beckoned the barkeeper for a bottle and two glasses, then Simon caught Henry Shepler's eye and beckoned him over.

Henry had hardly taken a seat when Simon blurted out what was presently uppermost in his mind. "Henry, the marshal here knows Pete Halder and Jake Moran, and he's seen dodgers on Gus Schilling." Having made that announcement Langley straightened in his chair, waited until the shuffling barkeeper had put down the bottle and glasses, then he ignored the whiskey to say also, " He'll take them off our hands."

Henry looked around. McDougal was eyeing Henry closely, evidently occupied with some private thoughts. " I'll leave Shepler's Spring on the morning stage heading north, Mister Shepler, and providin' you gents will furnish leg-irons and chains, I'll take those prisoners with me. The others are likely wanted somewhere, but I know three of them have bounties on them up north . . . Of course I could leave them here."

Henry sensed something. " Yeah, you could," he replied. " Then we'd have to feed 'em until we could get a law-officer to come down and get them."

" Maybe weeks, Mister Shepler."

Henry nodded, absolutely certain the lawman was leading up to something. Simon filled the pair of glasses, shoved one at McDougal, the other glass at Henry, who pushed it back as he said, " You've got something in mind, Marshal?"

" A trade, Mister Shepler. I'll take them out of here in chains on the morning stage . . . in exchange for my badge back."

Simon looked surprised but Henry did not lower his eyes from McDougal's face as he deliberately reached inside a shirt-pocket, tossed down the badge, then fished forth the limp, crumpled warrant for Bryce, and tossed that down too.

Simon was astonished. Then he started to redden. Neither the lawman nor the blacksmith looked at Langley. As McDougal reached to retrieve his badge he said, "Have you any idea what the penalty is for interfering with the work of a lawman, Mister Shepler, or for aidin' and abetting a fugitive so's he can escape?"

Henry's answer was short. "I found that badge and warrant. They were lyin' in the dirt over at the corral-yard." It was a bald lie. Henry did not feel as bad about telling it, as he had felt earlier when he had been deliberately evasive with McDougal. "Is there a penalty for findin' badges and warrants, Marshal?"

McDougal considered the badge on his palm without answering, then dropped it into the pocket Henry had taken it from and reached for the warrant, which he held in his fingers as he raised his eyes.

He ignored Henry's question and said, "You really figured you owed Bryce that much, didn't you?"

"Marshal, in my boots, what would you have done?"

"It's not much of a town, blacksmith."

"Maybe not, but we don't have a better one. They were going to ransack it then burn it."

McDougal tossed the useless warrant back in front of Henry Shepler. "Keep it for a souvenir, black-smith."

Henry was coming up to his feet when he picked up the folded paper and pocketed it. Then he nodded and turned away.

McDougal sat gazing at the retreating figure until it

passed from sight at the yonder doorway.

Simon, rummaging for something to say which might be appropriate, hit upon something. " Marshal, maybe you lost one, but you gained those others. I'd guess it to be a better'n even swap."

McDougal lifted his glass, emptied it, smiled at Simon and also started to arise. " You're right," he told Simon. " Five for one is a good trade. Now I've got to get some rest before stage-time in the morning." McDougal stood for a moment studying Simon as though he might have more to say, then turned away as though he had decided not to say it.

Outside, a dog barked in the roadway, there was a three-quarters moon, a rash of ice-chip stars and an immense, eerie ghost form of mountain north of the town, also eastward and westward.

The barking dog kept at it until the yapping mock of teasing coyotes running phantom-like just beyond the outskirts of town explained the dog's agitation.

Henry paused to make a smoke, then he surveyed the southward night, saw the lamp get snuffed out at the cafe, and got comfortable against a tie-rack a short distance from the saloon while he waited.

It was a fair wait, but when she appeared he forgot that. Anyway, he'd heard all his life that it took a woman at least three times as long to do something as it took a man.

The dog finally subsided, not willingly though, but because someone with an irate voice snarled him into silence. But nothing else was changed as they met, exchanged a smile then crossed to the west plank-walk and strolled on up through the village in the direction where he had seen her last night.

The coyotes were a distant, muted sound, a faint scent of wood-smoke lingered from the town's supper fires, day-long warmth against the earth was rising upward, bringing flower-scent with it, and as they left the plank-walk Elisabeth looked out where those crumpled mountains seemed miles closer than they were, and made a wide-flung gesture with her arms.

She turned her face to him in a smile of candid freedom as she said, "Doesn't it do that you, Mister Shepler?"

He smiled back, but uncertainly because he was uncertain what she was talking about.

"The clean fragrance, Mister Shepler, the high, magnificent mystery of those heavens, the endless beauty and serenity."

He looked at the sky, then at her. "I guess people feel those things different, Elisabeth. Men maybe notice them as much, but talk about them less than women. . . You hear the coyotes far off?"

She had heard them. "God's small creatures, Henry, with natural dignity, and innocence in their hearts."

He eyed her, gently rubbed the tip of his nose, and answered gently, "Yes, I expect so, but that innocence's got to do with a right sharp ability to scent up a hen-roost here in town, and that dignity's pretty darned underhanded and sneaky."

They made a wide half-circle, walking perhaps a mile

and a half, something Henry did not do under normal circumstances if it could be avoided, but he was enjoying it. She had a wholesome long stride, like a man's stride, and a supple, strong body which moved with muscular ease and perfect coordination. Of course there were endless things he would like to know about her.

She broke across his sombre thoughts. " It's the feeling of endless time, Henry. We need never act in haste about anything."

He nodded. Maybe not, maybe there was no hurry to know all the things he wanted to know. He watched her, felt her walking at his side, decided she was right, there was, indeed, no need for haste. The important thing was that she was vital, powerfully abundant and healthy.

Their hands brushed, brushed a second time and he felt for her fingers. She slowed her pace, slowed her thoughts and physical rhythm, became as inwardly absorbed as Henry also was.

Nothing was said until they were back in view of the main roadway, then, to make conversation, he told her of the federal deputy in town, of those men in the powder-house the federal officer would leave town with on the morning stage, and turned it over and over in his mind whether to confess what he had done about the badge and warrant, decided not to on the grounds that in the years ahead there would be plenty of time for them to confide in one another, and when her steps slackened even more, he willingly slowed too.

They were north-easterly of town a hundred or so

yards when she turned her head. He said nothing, which feminine intuition had told her the previous evening was his way, so she said, " Henry, do you think I ought to stay?"

His answer was slow. " Yes'm." He took a big breath. " *I* think so, but it's not up to me, is it?"

She stopped and faced him. " You—would have a lot to do with it."

He tightened his grip on her fingers. She responded, gently. " It'd make all the difference in the world if you'd stay, Elisabeth. To me, anyway."

She smiled. He was one of those men to whom putting feelings into words would always be difficult. To lighten the solemnity of the mood she said, " When Rosie returns, if you cared to we could make up a hamper of food and drive to the mountains."

He stood looking at her. He had not thought about a woman, especially one like Elisabeth, in a very long while. It had been even longer since he had thought of caring this hard, or of having someone care for him.

" Any time you want to go up there, I'll get the rig and be ready."

" The shop. . . ?"

" I can lock the doors easy as falling off a log."

She freed her fingers, took his arm and half turned him in the direction of town. In silence they walked back in close together.

Lauran Paine who, under his own name and various pseudonyms has written over 900 books, was born in Duluth, Minnesota. His family moved to California when he was at an early age and his apprenticeship as a Western writer came about through the years he spent in the livestock trade, rodeos, and even motion pictures—where he served as an extra because of his expert horsemanship in several films starring movie cowboy Johnny Mack Brown. In the late 1930s, Paine trapped wild horses in northern Arizona and, for a time, worked as a professional farrier. Paine came to know the old West through the eyes of many who had been born in the previous century and he learned that Western life had been very different from the way it was portrayed on the screen. "I knew men who had killed other men," he later recalled. "But they were the exceptions. Prior to and during the Depression, people were just too busy eking out an existence to indulge in Saturday-night brawls." He served in the U.S. Navy in the Second World War and began writing for Western pulp magazines following his discharge. It is interesting to note that all of his earliest novels (written under his own name and the pseudonym Mark Carrel) were published in the British market and he soon had as strong a following in that country as in the United States. Paine's Western fiction is characterized by strong plots, authenticity, an apparently effortless ability to construct situation and character, and a preference for building his stories upon a solid foundation of historical fact. *Adobe Empire* (1956), one of his best novels, is a fictionalized account of the last twenty years in the life of trader William Bent and, in an off-trail way, has a melancholy, bittersweet texture that is not easily forgotten. In later novels like *The White Bird* (1997) and *Cache Cañon* (1998), he showed that the special magic and power of his stories and characters had only matured along with his basic themes of changing times, changing attitudes, learning from experience, respecting Nature, and the yearning for a simpler, more moderate way of life. The film *Open Range* (Buena Vista, 2003), based on Paine's 1990 novel, starring Robert Duvall, Kevin Costner, and Annette Bening became an international success.